Arm Farm

by Sarah Butland

First Edition
ISBN 978-0-9811592-0-1

Published by:
ProSpec Industries Inc
PO Box 25100
Moncton, New Brunswick
E1C 9M9
Canada
http://www.ProSpecIndustries.com

ProSpec Industries Inc books are available at special discounts for bulk purchases for sales promotions, fundraising, or educational use.

Special editions or book excerpts can also be created to specification upon request.

For more information about the author,
Sarah Butland, please visit:
http://www.SarahButland.com

With many thanks to

Trent Washburn and his many hours of perfecting an unseen Arm Farm and making it as beautiful as such a farm can be.

My family and friends for their critique, edits and patience while making Natalie's story the best it can be.

Sarah Heiman, my editor, who surpassed my expectations and unreasonable time restraint. She came through in a pinch and blew me away.

My fans, for without you my voice would never be heard.

ProSpec Industries Inc for dealing with my high expectations and meeting them all.

And, of course, my husband and son for the love they mirror.

Enjoy your time at the

Arm Farm

Chapter 1

As I walked through the valley of the shadow of arms, I quickened my pace to just less than a jog. For better clarity and my own sanity I felt my first visit should have been during daylight; instead my professor insisted on meeting at dawn, knowing I was always early for appointments. It was still dark, with the sun barely above the horizon, and rain clouds threatened to make me even less comfortable. My professor was late, as he often was, but he always thought it was OK as long as he apologized.

Looking around me I understood exactly what my professor had warned me to expect. Arms grew out of the ground like dandelions in the summer, only they weren't bright with petals; they were dreary with disturbing protrusions. It certainly wasn't like any forest I'd ever seen. Even the books didn't depict the finality of the Arm Farm, which was sinking in quickly.

Save for the sinewy arms against the dreary backdrop and the random chirp from faraway birds, I was alone. The only immediate sounds were my footsteps, the pounding of my heart, and quiet words. I was confused — unsure of where the words were coming from — but listening more closely, suddenly realized that it was me praying.

"…Stay inside me as I dare to tread, be beside me in case I stumble. Dear God, guide me through this…"

Unfortunately, this was the first moment I had ever put my trust in God so I found it difficult to believe He would suddenly appear. Years without feeling His presence wasn't a strong indication that He would suddenly take an interest in me, because He had done me so wrong when I was a little girl that I found it difficult to let myself embrace His existence.

Without much looking around I knew I had found the right tree where our meeting was to take place. It appeared exactly like the professor had described; it was hard to miss a tree shaped like a 'D'. Looking at the tree's void of branches and foliage I sat right in its belly, which offered only a bit more comfort and safety than one of its protruding limbs. I was slightly shocked at the health of all the trees despite the bombardment of decomposing appendages. There wasn't a barn or any livestock in sight, not a sound to hear without straining. I was left to my own devices with only my imagination, which too often played cruel tricks on me. The text books discourage wild flights of imagination, but those *in* the field embrace them. Harder than any test my professor could offer was my own task of learning to embrace — and control — my wild imagination.

The hands below began waving at me; the arms with missing hands were swaying despite the lack of wind. Sinew had collected on each protruding arm and swayed softly in the light, warm breeze. My own hand began to tremble and I began trying to concentrate on calming the shakes away, but they insisted on staying. I wouldn't give up trying. One by one the waving hands began to point at me and then seemed to turn to point to an approaching vehicle that looked nothing like the professor's. My nerves peaked, and then relaxed when I saw a familiar face emerge from the red PT Cruiser.

"Professor!" I shouted, knowing he could only barely hear me, but wanting to make his presence concrete in order to slow my racing heart. I thought about running to him, but decided that the professional thing to do would be to wait. My trembles had reduced to a minimum and I remained seated on the tree. The professor, dressed simply in tight, dark-colored jeans and an old plaid sweater, strode more confidently than I had a few minutes prior. His hair was combed much like he wore it at school, but he looked much more at ease than I had ever had the pleasure of seeing.

"Natalie, you made it. Terrific! And punctual as usual. I know you won't want to spend your whole Saturday here, so let's get started whenever you're ready."

The professor's light blue eyes peered at me like he had known me all of his life. I sensed we were starting to become more than teacher and student — and I liked it.

"Ready and waiting. Thanks again for this opportunity. I realize you probably don't want to spend your entire day with me here either, not to mention that you're teaching for free."

"It's no trouble at all. I love teaching when I know the student is absorbing the material. Besides, I can only teach so much in class and you are the only student who realizes this. You have a lot of potential and I want to embrace that. Just remember me when you've made it to the big league."

Despite the chill in the air, my face flushed; Professor Matthews was the only teacher who could do that to me. I realized that he noticed my embarrassment even though he tried to conceal his knowledge.

"I trust you brought your tools," he said.

Jumping down from my perch, I stumbled over the top of my bag and Professor Matthews saw what broke my fall. Great, my second embarrassment that day — not that I was keeping track. Opening my backpack, I pulled out a notebook and my forensic evidence kit as he pointed to the nearest protruding arm and asked me to get started. When I bent down to get a closer look, I was startled by the smell emanating from the test area; Professor Matthews noticed my reaction.

Chapter 2

My hands shook and I clamped one to my mouth to block the sudden bile rising from my stomach, fighting to escape. To the disapproval of my stomach, I forced it back down and brought my tweezers and test tube to the rotting arm. As I tried to be nonchalant, I saw Professor Matthews' grin out of the corner of my eye. I was already flustered enough not to worry about blushing. Taking a deep breath through my mouth, I completed my task as his husky but clear voice filled the creepy silence.

"That odor was always there, you're just becoming attuned to it at the closer position. You won't believe me but by the end of the day the smell will no longer be an issue. Do remember that each corpse in its varying stage of decomposition and condition will have its own distinct smell. What you smell right here is not necessarily the worst of it. I'm not trying to lecture you — I'll save that for the entire class. As you know, crime scene investigators who haven't seen all stages set up the Arm Farm. That way we can catalog differences of decomposition and compare them with actual crime scenes. Doing this tells us a lot about time frame and how nature can tamper with evidence."

A low rumble sounded in the distance. I looked around, afraid it would rain, and felt like I was being watched. *The Farm sure does play tricks on its visitors*, I thought.

"When you're called to a scene, the evidence will have been left by the killer, not a scientist. The possibilities are endless when you're in the field."

Lacking words, I ignored the moment of silence and quickly finished my preliminary examination. "Done." Reading from my notebook, I explained the arm owner's estimated age and race, and my personal insight on how this arm came to be rotting here. The cause of death, of course, could not be proven without the rest of the body.

"Excellent, but you missed something."

I thought for only a second. "Oh, right, the fingernails. I examined them, but I just didn't report what I found."

"Always report all of your findings, or lack thereof. You may not think a certain piece of information is important but you have yet to put the puzzle together. If you're missing pieces, you will never be able to see the whole picture."

"I'm sorry, it's still too early in the day for me." I knew the excuse was lame and felt terrible for saying it. I quickly continued, "I found quite a bit of dirt under the nails. At a crime scene I would bag it and bring it in for analysis, but I will leave it here for the next guy to miss."

"Good work, CSI Hartman, now on to the next one."

I gathered my tools and followed where Professor Matthews directed. By the second arm I was breathing through my nose, not noticing the putrid smell — I was a natural.

The rest of the morning continued in much the same manner until my stomach grumbled. Third embarrassment. Professor Matthews offered to break for lunch and I eagerly accepted. Maybe too eagerly, in hindsight. As we walked back to our cars we agreed on a restaurant where we'd have lunch, and we continued our chat as he locked the gates to the Arm Farm. I gave him back the key he'd lent me for entry and we got into our separate cars. On the way, I called my friend Amanda.

"Hi Amanda, how are you? I know we had plans for today but I'll have to reschedule." I sounded nervous and she knew it. I couldn't hide anything from her, but she seemed too distracted to pry any more than she did.

"No biggie, but why? Do you have a date?"

"Yes and no. Amanda, you can't repeat this to anyone and I don't have time to explain. Professor Matthews took me out to the Arm Farm and is now treating me to lunch."

"Nat, that's awesome! The lunch, I mean. The Farm idea freaks me out."

"It's nothing." It didn't feel like nothing, but I tried to play things cool. I could only imagine what Amanda was thinking after I hung up the phone. She was the only one who knew how I was beginning to feel about Professor Matthews. Admittedly, I couldn't even decide how to feel, yet she was with me every step of the way — sometimes even a step ahead. But we both knew I had to move past those feelings.

The professor and I arrived at the Meet and Griddle and I drove around the parking lot, scouring for people I recognized, before pulling in to a spot. I hoped no one from school would see us together, but Professor Matthews didn't seem to mind.

While the professor and the waiter chose a table I excused myself to go to the restroom. I needed to clean up and I also used the opportunity to scan for familiar faces on my way through the restaurant. No one I recognized caught my eye. The restroom was as spotless as the restaurant alluded, and it was mortifying to realize, as I walked by the reassuringly empty stalls, how disgusting I must have smelled. I hoped I wouldn't ruin any of the other diners' appetites.

By the time I returned, Professor Matthews had already ordered for me. A glass of red wine stood alone at my table setting. "What's this?"

"I thought we'd celebrate our findings. I hope red wine is OK and that you're also not allergic to shellfish."

"I love seafood, thank you, but what did we find?"

"I found — or, we — found your niche, your talent, when you found the evidence." Not used to hearing compliments or even references to having talents, I blushed for a fourth time that day. "I can count on one hand all the students I felt the need to test at the Farm. Three of them made it past the gate without vomiting, and one made it through the entire day without retching. You've already completed all of the tasks I've set without a word of complaint."

"That first arm almost got me, and you didn't see how I did when I arrived."

"And you've aced all the tests until now. I was at the Farm before you, you know. I watched you hesitate at the gate and saw you contemplate sitting on the ground or remain standing. I…" His voice trailed off as he saw the look of astonishment on my face.

I couldn't decide between slapping him, leaving him, or hugging him, but the smell of the arriving lunch paralyzed me into inaction. The waiter left and the tension returned.

Even the best and most observant could miss important facts. Having watched Natalie since she was a baby, I stepped up my own game when she began making decisions that could affect me. I could have been sitting at the same table, yet she wouldn't have seen me no matter how hard she tried. Within earshot I sat and worried.

I felt proud of her accomplishments but fearful of them as well.

Chapter 3

"Let me explain before you jump to any drastic conclusions."

"Too late, Professor Matthews, my mind is already made up." I reached for my purse and began to stand despite my grumbling stomach. When he reached out his arm and pulled me back I noticed his strength. My frustration stifled any other feeling from rushing in.

"Reacting without knowing all the facts is not a good thing for what you're studying to become. You need to take in all of the details before drawing your conclusions. The primary reason that I watched you was to confirm my belief in you. Even though you failed to complete the process of securing the scene by confirming no one was there before you or using your crime scene tape around the perimeter, I think you are ready." I sat back in my chair and skeptically asked what he thought I was ready for.

"When appropriate, I can select an outstanding student to attend an advancement conference hosted by professional forensic scientists for people already working in the field. The school would finance everything as long as you're willing to attend a few press conferences before and after the event. With your consent of course, I would be honored to submit your name."

"Professor Matthews, you can't be serious?"

"Couldn't be more."

Ever since I was a little girl, I had dreamed of attending the Science in U conference and kept track of who's who in the forensic field. Science in U was commonly held at Disney World; I had to ask before I went speechless. "Is it in Florida?"

"The happiest place on earth," he replied with a grin.

"Are Stephen Pratt and Krista Munz teaching it?"

"They are. They always take that week off to teach it. They are always on call for field work, so if there's an emergency you may be able to join them and see how they work. Let's hope that doesn't happen though, because we know that would mean there are more murders than the regular force can handle."

Almost choking on my food, I quickly made two very wise decisions. The first was to put my fork down and the second was to agree to attend the conference. Professor Matthews looked genuinely pleased with my second decision, not realizing the severity of the first, and ordered another bottle of wine. I asked if he was trying to get me drunk. He assured me that he wasn't, however, after a few more drinks I did feel extremely light-headed. I couldn't drive feeling the way I did.

Fifth.

With the second bottle of wine and our meals finished, we agreed it was time to pay the bill and get some fresh air. Professor Matthews — not being one to miss anything, whether obvious or subtle — noticed my waver as we stood.

"I don't mind quitting for the day and driving you home. I promise to try to make things as comfortable for you as possible."

"But my car…I'll just call my friends to come get me and the car. Thank you for today, you've been very kind," I slurred while trying to be subtle.

"It's been my pleasure, Natalie. Thank you for accepting the invitations I offered."

"Invitations?"

"First to visit me at the Farm, then to go to the conference. I know you'll take a lot away from both."

"Oh, yes, but for now I need to sleep this off." And then Professor Matthews made his exit. I was left alone in a crowded restaurant with blurred vision, cloudy judgment, and a few regrets. A stranger approached me in the lobby and helped me sit down. I heard myself mumble something about calling a friend and was surprised when the stranger handed me his cell phone.

My intentions were to call Amanda but I couldn't see her memorized number through the fog and gave up. The man took his phone back from my hands and asked me a question. My face must have told him what I wasn't able to say.

"Is there anyone we can call for you?" The stranger asked at a pace I could understand.

"Amanda Witt, with two 'T's. She's in the phone book." I was embarrassed that I could remember to instruct him of all the relevant information, yet couldn't recall Amanda's phone number. "It's 617-something."

"Here it is." Through blurred vision I saw him dialing the number and then bring the phone to his ear. "Hi, Amanda? You don't know me but I'm calling about your friend…"

"Natalie," I offered.

"Natalie. She's unable to drive and is requesting that you and a friend come to pick her up and her car."

I always found Amanda loud on the phone but her screeching was even louder and unusually clear this time, giving me a headache. "Oh my God, what happened? Professor Matthews…Where is she? Where is he?" Under different circumstances I would have laughed at the fact that I heard her every word.

"Natalie is in the entrance to the Meat and Griddle. Her guest is nowhere to be seen."

"That jerk. I'll be there in ten minutes. Tell her not to go anywhere."

"She won't, and thanks."

The stranger made his exit after explaining that my friend would be there soon. "Thank you, you've been very kind," I stammered.

Amanda and her boyfriend Gary arrived in eight minutes, and in that time I managed to avoid making a mess of the restaurant lobby. Unfortunately, I did receive a few glares and turned away some business. Gary spoke first.

"I'll take your car back to the apartment and let you girls catch up. Where are your keys?"

"Thanks Gary, here they are." It actually took Amanda steadying my arm for me to be able to hand him the keys. I remembered the prof telling me that he wasn't trying to get me drunk and yet here I was. *I* knew it was my fault, but I had to enlighten my friend.

"Come on, sweetie, let's go home. What did that son of a bitch do to you? He seemed like such a sweet guy."

"He is. There's a story behind this," I wanted to quickly squash any harsh judgments. The fresh air hit me like a windshield surprises a bird and I fell. Amanda would have fallen with me, but I had enough sense to let go of her hand. "The restaurant won't be letting me back in any time soon," I managed to say.

"I don't need to hear the story now. I'll take you to my place, where I can watch you."

Chapter 4

It took much more than eight minutes for the return trip, for which I was grateful. Any faster and I would have stained Amanda's car interior, so I am sure that she was grateful too.

We arrived and Amanda immediately escorted me to her bed, where I slept the afternoon away. Upon awakening, I saw a table set with steaming soup and a glass of milk. Amanda was sitting quietly in the corner, so her question startled me as it broke the silence.

"Uh...yeah, I do feel a bit better, thanks. I feel horrible for ruining your plans, I didn't know who else to call."

"Don't be ridiculous. We weren't doing anything anyway. Gary was itching to find any excuse to go out, so it all worked out on this end. But what about you? What happened?"

"Thank you, the soup is delicious. This is just what I needed. We went to the Arm Farm because Professor Matthews wanted to give me some one-on-one time, professionally speaking. Things were going great, so when he invited me to lunch I was more than happy to go. I didn't lose all of my senses though — I convinced him that it was best we take separate cars.

"He ordered wine and I managed to drown my nervousness without much thought to counting the glasses."

"But why did he buy wine when you were both driving?"

"Oh my, I forgot all about that. He's sending me to a conference — *the* conference. He thinks I'm good enough to meet the best in the field. And it's at Disney World!"

"Congratulations, Nat! Isn't this what you've been dreaming of since childhood?"

"Absolutely! Now is everything more clear?"

"Yes, that's awesome, Natalie. Wait, when do you go? Can you bring a guest? What do you need me to do?" She seemed to be just as thrilled as I was and the wine fiasco was forgotten.

"Honestly, I was looped before I could think to ask. The professor must think I'm an idiot. I'll call him tomorrow and ask him, as well as apologize. He was such a gentleman the entire day and I acted the fool."

"Don't worry about it. He's just your teacher, not a boyfriend. Monday will be awkward but that'll pass. Where should we celebrate tonight?"

The look on my face made her pause; I just couldn't stomach celebrating twice in the same day despite the importance of the event. "I'll take a rain check but I would love to go out with you before I leave town. I'll have a better idea of when we can celebrate once I talk to the prof."

"I'm going to hold you to that, I promise."

"I'm counting on it. Now that you've fed me and nursed me back to health, do you mind driving me home?"

"Of course not, but are you sure you want to be alone right now? We could rent some chick flicks and talk boy stuff until we fall asleep. You could even borrow some of my PJ's and I can ask Gary to sleep at a friend's. It'll be like we're ten again."

"I really need a bath, but I just bought the new Adam Sandler movie. Have you seen it? It's supposed to be a side-splitter. Why don't you take me home, and then you kill some time for a bit while I bathe? That way Gary can sleep in his own bed."

"Sounds great, just let me grab a few things and call him to let him know where I'll be."

"No hurry, and Amanda, thanks again."

"What are friends for?"

How many times had she said that since we were toddlers? A lot more than I had. Despite being the conscientious one, it seemed that I was somehow the one who was always in trouble. If Amanda taught me anything, which she did, it was to embrace life by taking risks. I was still stuck on only taking calculated risks but they were definitely paying off — finally!

I would have never applied to university if Amanda hadn't already been accepted. She'd almost had to fill out the application for me, because no one else would have done it. Amanda eventually convinced me that I had nothing to lose and my dream to gain, so I swallowed the lump and went for it.

After two months, two *grueling* months, I had received an envelope from my top choice school. I had been too nervous to open it alone so I called Amanda at work. She came home immediately, hugging me before grabbing the envelope. She tore it open and asked if I wanted her to read the letter first. I told her to read it out loud but I didn't hear a word of it; her expression had told me the news.

Amanda's question brought me back to the present. "Natalie, are you ready?"

"Sorry, I was just remembering the day I was accepted into school. We celebrated in much the same way as I did today, only the last time it started with cheap beer."

"Those were good times. What am I going to do when you're off solving crimes and I'm still trying to figure out what I'm working towards? A peanut butter sandwich just isn't the same without bread."

"It won't be so bad, Amanda. I'll never forget about you and I don't plan to go very far."

"You will go far, maybe not in distance but professionally speaking. Let's not talk about that now. We're celebrating and only thinking happy thoughts tonight. Ready?"

"Sure am. That soup did wonders. I'll need the recipe."

It didn't take long to arrive at my place even though Amanda insisted on staying under the speed limit. Only remnants remained of what I felt earlier, but I was still determined to run a hot bath to eliminate my awful stench. Approaching the driveway, we were surprised to see that Gary had already delivered my car safely.

As I walked by the driver's side door, my eye caught something on the seat. Thinking that Gary had left the keys there, I bent down to retrieve them but was startled to discover a package of nicotine gum.

Chapter 5

"This must have fallen out of Gary's pocket. I didn't know he was quitting."

"I didn't think he was. That's great though — his smoking has always been a sore spot with us. It's weird that he's been keeping his quitting from me. Maybe he's just not doing well with it."

"He'll regret dropping the evidence now, won't he? Come on in, my friend, excuse the mess."

"Oh, I'm used to it. We have lived together, remember?"

"Every day. Help yourself to a beer or something in the fridge if you can find anything worthwhile. I shouldn't be long."

"Take as long as you need, it has been an exciting day for you."

"You're right about that."

I left Amanda rummaging through my cupboards while I readied my bath and found some appropriate pajamas. By the time I got into the bath, Amanda had made a decision.

"I'm going out to get something to eat, Nat, anything in mind?"

"Chinese would be excellent. Get some extra wontons and sweet and sour sauce. Just grab some money from my purse, I should have enough."

"Haven't had wontons in a while, great choice. I'll be back before you're out." She ignored my offer to pay.

The last I heard was the door closing before I entered my solitary world: a fantastic world I created to escape the usual humdrum life I led. I entered the world less often now than I had in childhood and had almost convinced myself that I no longer needed it. Unfortunately, quitting a long-established habit was not an easy task.

In my world I often saw myself with my parents, laughing and loving, but that day was different. As I dozed off, I saw the trees from the Arm Farm. I let my guard down until I realized the trees were growing knives instead of leaves. I took off running toward the Arm Farm exit. I couldn't actually run as fast as I always did in dreams, but the tree was always just over my shoulder.

I stumbled, and when I got up I saw some hands beckoning me. As stupid as your typical dreamer, I followed their instruction. There was a tool kit beside the arm that the hands were directing me to, so I began analyzing the arm. The lines, the slender but sinewy fingers, and the olive fingernail polish told me that I was taking evidence from my long-dead mother's hand.

I was so hot on the Farm that I was oblivious to the dropping temperature of the still water. It wasn't until I heard someone enter my apartment that I realized where I was. I trembled from the transition to reality and from the chilled water. I dressed and slowly opened the door, relieved to see that Amanda was the intruder and that she was carrying Chinese food.

"Smells good."

"Me or the food? I'm starving, you ready?"

"Just have to brush my hair but it should only take a second. I just have to find my brush." Oddly, I couldn't find the brush anywhere and gave up trying before my food got cold. Instead, I used the travel brush in my purse.

Adam Sandler and Chinese food were just what I needed, and when Amanda said she was going to go home I was too exhausted to object. She had a lot of things to do in the morning so she had decided not to spend the night. The phone rang as I watched Amanda get into her car.

I answered the phone. "What did you forget?"

"Sorry?"

"Oh, Gary, I thought it was your other half. Look, thanks again for dropping my car off — I owe you."

"It was no problem, really. When does Amanda plan to be back?"

"About five minutes, she just left. Oh, and she has your Nicorette. You must have dropped it when you got out of the car. I hope it works out for you."

"My what?"

"Your gum, it was on the seat. I thought it was my car keys at first. Do you still have my keys?"

"I left them in the glove compartment, but the gum...oh, never mind. Amanda's here so I'll let you go."

I found the conversation very suspicious, especially since Amanda couldn't possibly be home already, but decided it was nothing. If the gum wasn't Gary's...but it had to be. Remembering Professor Matthews's advice about not jumping to any conclusions, the situation wouldn't settle. I slept on it but decided to call Amanda in the morning.

"Sleep well?"

"Like a bear in winter, you?"

"I won't sleep well until I come back from the conference. I'm just so excited! As soon as I'm finished talking to you I'm going to call the professor. I think he goes to church, so I called you first."

"Well, call me back when you find out all the goods about the conference, I am curious to know. Oh, I should tell you my good news. I talked to Gary last night about the gum. It was his."

Jackpot.

"He was going to surprise me for my birthday."

Wait, that's not right.

"I'm so proud of him."

I'm not. Not knowing what to say, I changed the subject and then rushed her off the phone. To me, Gary seemed startled at the mention of the gum but to Amanda he quickly took ownership. My gut was telling me that the Nicorette was not Gary's and I recalled Matthews' words of wisdom to the class: "If you have an opportunity to use your tools, use them. It will prevent most of you from losing them." I determined that I had the tools to confirm whether the gum was Gary's, so I should make use of them.

I checked my car for any other significant evidence the culprit may have left and found a hair stuck in the headrest of the driver's seat. I also swabbed the steering wheel for sweat stains, and then I brought everything inside.

Chapter 6

I laid the evidence on the table and eyed my phone, then decided to call the professor while reviewing the evidence.

"Professor Matthews, it's Natalie."

"Natalie! I was just thinking about you, how are you feeling?"

"Anxious, curious, excited, but standing on my own two feet so much better than yesterday. I don't remember if you told me many details about the conference so I was calling for those."

"I thought you would and I am willing to give you all the info I have. Unfortunately, it's not much yet. Let me see, the conference is going to be held from the eighteenth to the twentieth —"

"Of this month? But today's the…" I checked my watch to confirm my assumption, "…seventh!"

"I know, it's short notice but I had to make absolutely sure that you were ready. And, Natalie, I'm very glad — and sure — that you are."

"Me, too. Am I able to bring a friend? And when do I leave?"

"Science in U does provide a plane ticket for you and a guest, but they haven't purchased the tickets yet. They are closed today so I'll call and announce the news to them tomorrow. Then they will give me the schedule and all other information. If you'd like, I could take you out to dinner tomorrow night to go over everything."

Still counting the embarrassing moments. "Sure, my last class is over at five and then I'm free."

We arranged to meet at my place at 5:30 p.m. the next day. I explained where I lived and ended the call. I gave myself a second to celebrate and then got back to business.

After processing the evidence from my car, I realized I had nothing to compare it to and documented "inconclusive" in my report. I wouldn't, and couldn't, let it go. I called Amanda.

"We forgot to eat dessert last night. If you're not busy, I can come over and share what the professor told me."

"I've been craving dessert! Come on over."

I grabbed a cake out of the fridge and began to search for my car keys when I remembered that Gary had left them in the glove compartment. I found them where he promised he'd left them, and when I took them out of the compartment, an unknown object caught my eye. I reached back into the glove compartment and pulled out a small envelope.

Opening the envelope, I was shocked to see a small card and I immediately looked for the signature — a secret admirer; perfect.

Because my car had been left unlocked, the possibilities were endless; my immediate guess was Gary. But why would he leave such a thing? Our relationship had ended years ago, and he was with Amanda now. Were he and Amanda having problems that I wasn't aware of? With these questions on the forefront of my mind the visit was going to be awkward, but Amanda was waiting.

Gary opened the door when I arrived and although I tried to act as if nothing happened, it was obvious to him that something was up.

"Amanda just went out to get milk. I thought it would give us a chance to talk," Gary said.

"I really have nothing to say to you. You know how I feel about her."

"I know and that's what makes this so hard. But you told me that you owed me one and I want to cash in. Please, I reacted badly about the gum and would take my reaction back if I could. I already talked to Amanda about the gum and she's taking it amazingly well. Let's not dwell on it and make things worse."

"But we're so close."

"Which is why you don't want to hurt her." The door opened and almost hit me, so I stepped out of the way. "That was quick, Amanda. Natalie just arrived."

"Oh good, we just realized that we were out of milk. You can't have any kind of chocolate without milk."

"Got that right." I took off my shoes and excused myself to set the cake on the counter. I took a quick peek at the couple and when I saw that they were not watching me, made my way to the bathroom and closed the door. I hoped to find Gary's brush so that I could take a piece of hair for future comparison if the situation escalated. I found his brush right away and bagged a few hair samples. I then dug in my purse for fingerprinting tools and took a print from his brush. When I heard the clatter of dishes, I quickly put everything away.

Before leaving the bathroom I flushed the toilet and washed my hands, careful to put the brush back where I'd found it. Neither Gary nor Amanda seemed to notice my absence and I left later that night with the evidence, minus any confrontation.

I sped on the way home, anxious to put the mystery of the secret admirer to rest — or at least part of it. After I received the answer to this problem, I would know my next course of action. Unfortunately, the answer only ended up forcing me to ask more questions.

Even though my test kit results would not hold up in court, they would be extremely accurate. I tested the samples three times just to confirm, and determined that the hairs from my car and the hairs from Gary's brush were not from the same head. The fingerprints were circumstantial evidence at best because they matched only three Galton points, needing twelve to hold up in court, and the minutiae — the details left by the ridges of a fingerprint — was smudged.

I began to slip into my solitary refuge to forget about everything when my cat suddenly jumped in front of me. Usually an independent cat, being obvious was his way of telling me that someone was outside my apartment. Not expecting anyone, I was curious and went to the window, where I saw nothing but an empty balcony and a full moon. I fed Whiskers, called him a fool and crawled into bed.

Sleep didn't come easily but whether my insomnia stemmed from excitement or curiosity, I'll never know. When my eyes finally shut completely, the alarm opened them again. I had to get ready for school.

I had Professor Matthews for my second class, which Gary attended as well. If I wasn't nervous about my upcoming trip, I was nervous about being with Gary. I believe my shaky nerves were a combination of both scenarios. The first class, biology, went by in a blur. I chose to arrive early to my next class, figuring being late would create more of a spectacle.

"Natalie, you're early. You must be excited." It seemed Professor Matthews was waiting for me, and I couldn't help but wonder if I was just being paranoid.

"Very excited! Going to Science in U is what I've always wanted."

"Me too, so I'll pick you up at 5:30 p.m.? I don't want the other classmates to know we're going to dinner, so let's keep it quiet. They might think I'm playing favorites and we do not want that."

Why was he so excited about my honor that he was rambling? I wondered. It was almost as if he were the one going. "Have you ever attended the Science in U conference?"

Professor Matthews chuckled and said yes just as another student entered and our conversation was cut short. Moments later the room was full and class started. The professor waited until the end of the class period to make his announcement about selecting me to attend Science in U. Gary was the first to congratulate me by giving me a hug. I subtly squeezed him back and thanked him, turning to the next well-wisher in line, but Gary's question stopped me.

Chapter 7

"Is this why you're practicing on my things?"
"Sorry?"
"My brush. Amanda noticed fingerprint dust on it. Don't worry, I told her I practiced taking prints on my own brush, but I was wondering why you did it. Now I understand."
"Yeah...I need as much practice as possible," I said, thinking quickly — hopefully quickly enough. "I compared the prints to the ones I took from my keys from the other day: a perfect match." Concerned with why Gary would think he should cover for me, I thought of comparing the brush print to a new sample from a fingerprint on my keys or door handle, because the one from the door handle may not have been his.

Gary walked away and the next classmate in line approached me: Mike, a returning student who already had experience in the field but was on suspension from working with the police — apparently he didn't only come on too strong with me. He had decided to refresh his knowledge and was in most of my classes. He was a quiet man who seemed to pay very close attention in class, but often asked me to help review his notes with him. I always politely declined because I was uncomfortable with the fact that I was the only classmate he asked, and he then made A's on everything despite my refusal to help. He knew his stuff and he was coming on way too strong for my liking. This exchange was no different.

Sarah Butland

"Congratulations. I knew you'd be picked to go to Science in U. I can't wait to catch up when you get back, say...over dinner?"

"Mike, I do have to decline, but I will be giving a presentation in class to let everyone know what I learned. Have a good day." I couldn't bear faking another civil conversation with the other students waiting to congratulate me — they had never spoken to me before — so I excused myself and went to lunch.

I was the talk of the school for the remainder of the day, which embarrassed me beyond belief. The day went by in a fog and I was home before I realized my classes were over. I called Amanda to update her on the day's happenings and was devastated to hear her crying. She didn't cry often but I could picture her pouty lips, glistening dark eyes, and the way she'd be holding her hands over them. As sad as it was, she was gorgeous when she cried.

"What's wrong?" She tried to cover up the fact that she was crying, so I was forced to pry. "Did something happen? Is it Gary?"

"Just...it's nothing. I'm just having a horrible day. I'm glad you called though. Tell me everything."

"I actually called with good news, I think. I wanted to officially invite you to go with me to Disney World. I really wouldn't be able to stand that much time with anyone else."

"Oh Natalie, thank you. Oh no...what week is it again?" I told her and heard her shuffling through papers. "Shit, that's next week and I'm taking midterms. I really can't afford to miss them."

"Can't you talk to your profs and arrange to take your midterms when we get back? All of my professors are rescheduling mine, but, then again, I was the one asked to attend the conference and it's something that will help me tremendously more than taking a few tests. This is a once-in-a-lifetime opportunity, and I'd hate to see you miss out on the free trip."

"I'll talk to my professors but I doubt it'll help. You might want to think of someone else just in case. I have French class with Madame Gilles first thing tomorrow, so I will let you know what she says. Her exam is the most important and she's the least likely to change things for me."

"But who else would I bring? You're my best friend..."

"I know that Gary has been itching to have a vacation and because he takes forensics classes he'll understand what you'll be talking about after the workshops. I really wouldn't mind. I trust you both. Besides, you've been there and done him before and I know you don't regret breaking it off with him. Lucky for me."

The doorbell rang and surprised me. Looking at my watch, I realized that it was 5:30 p.m. already. I didn't have time to change so I told Amanda that I'd think about taking Gary, but that I had to go. I grabbed my coat and purse and opened the door.

"Sorry, I was caught on the phone and didn't realize it was so late. Any place in particular in mind? Do I need to change?"

"It's a surprise, but you're beau— you're fine, no need to change. Ready?"

That was the seventh time the professor made me blush but I turned to close the door before he could see. "I am. Let's go."

When we arrived at the restaurant, I felt underdressed and told him so.

"Rubbish, you're fine, people are staring at you because they know how special you are. They probably also can't believe that you're with lowly old me."

"You're not old, Professor Matthews —"

"But I am lowly and tonight, by the way, it's Brian, not Professor Matthews. That will help in your attempt at convincing me that I'm not old."

The waiter appeared and I placed my order, insisting on sparkling water in place of wine. Brian did the same. We made small talk until the food arrived and when it did, we both devoured it as if we hadn't eaten for months. Neither of us commented on the haste.

"Business time?"

"Of course," he said bending down to retrieve a briefcase, which I only then noticed for the first time that night. It seemed I was oblivious to almost everything since he had told me the news. He glanced at his papers and then at his Timex before continuing.

"It seems like I'm trying to master the art of short notice. Your first press conference is tomorrow morning."

"What? You're kidding, right? I've never been the center of attention at a media event. I've *been* to some, but how do I know what questions to prepare for? What do I wear? And my classes — I shouldn't miss any more than I have to..." Brian reached his hand out to stop me.

"Natalie, you'll be fine. I've made up a list of possible questions, which of course may or may not be asked. I've already spoken with all of your teachers, but you'll need to ask someone else about what to wear."

Eighth.

"Of course, sorry, it's just that everything seems to be happening so quickly and I haven't caught up yet."

"I'm really sorry. I would have told you sooner, but there were hurdles I had to get through first. If I could have, I would have told you that we were even considering sending you. But, I know you're ready for it and I'm more than willing to help you when I can. Here's my list of questions. Actually, give me a second."

He was up and gone before I could grab the list, so I decided to take the opportunity to visit the ladies' room. I wasn't gone for long but when I returned, it looked like I was walking into the middle of a press conference. Brian ran up to me to explain.

"We're going to have a practice run. The restaurant is wonderfully accommodating and so are its guests. You ready?" I must have nodded, as he then proceeded to introduce me to the room. I walked to the makeshift podium and did what came naturally.

"Thank you for coming, I'm sorry if I seem a little off today, but this has been so exciting for me. Well, since this isn't a lecture I'll open the floor for your questions. Yes, the gentleman in the blue."

"What do you hope you'll accomplish at this conference, and what do you hope you'll take with you?" He read from a card Brian must have given him.

It felt appropriate to begin with a bit of humor, so I did. "What I truly hope to come back with is a really nice tan —" I paused for laughter, "— but seriously, I've always dreamed of being in the forensics field and I hope that this conference will improve my chances of that."

"Have you heard of Dr. Henry Lee, and if you have, are you excited to meet him?"

I turned to Brian as I said that, yes, I'd heard of Dr. Lee. I then asked Brian if Dr. Lee would be attending the conference.

"Yes, the last I've heard he plans to attend," Brian confirmed.

"Wow, I guess I'll be more than happy to meet him. Of course I will try to be professional and sophisticated when I do."

The mock press conference continued on like that until Brian finally ended the test run by saying that I needed my sleep for the real thing. I thanked everyone who remained for helping me, and they offered their congratulations and best wishes. Brian drove me home and offered to pick me up in the morning.

"I do appreciate everything you've done for me but I'm going to decline your offer. I think driving over by myself will be much more relaxing."

"If you change your mind, you know my number. I'm being interviewed too, so I'll be there anyway." After giving me the details of when and where to meet, he wished me luck again, got into his car, and drove off.

Chapter 8

The phone was ringing as I was opening my door and I reached it just in time. "I was just about to call you, I just got in from dinner with Brian, er…the prof."

"First name basis, huh? What's going on with you two that you're not telling me?"

"Nothing, Amanda, he's just helping me with everything. After dinner he created a makeshift press conference because I have my first one in the morning. I need your help in choosing what to wear. Can you come over?"

"I know just the thing for you. It's in my closet so I'll bring it right over." She hung up before I could say another word.

The outfit that Amanda brought me was better than suitable and fit me perfectly. She knew how conservative I was, and since we were the same size she brought over her most recently purchased pantsuit. With a scalloped neckline and short sleeves, the beige blouse fit my upper body like a glove. Although the color looked much better with Amanda's stark black hair color it matched nicely with my own sandy brown. The darker brown pants flared beautifully over the beige flats I intended to wear. I hated to say it, but I looked good! I asked Amanda if she'd had a chance to talk to her teachers and she replied that she hadn't. I invited her to the press conference, told her what time it began, and she accepted. Her first class started an hour after the event and she explained that she might have to leave early, so she would take her own car.

I arrived at the press conference venue well in advance on Tuesday, a good forty-five minutes early, with little sleep because I was too scared of what dreams I may have had if I slept too long. When I got there I saw that a few reporters had already assembled. I avoided them as much as I could, which became more difficult once one of them recognized me. It wasn't too long after that when I saw Amanda and Professor Matthews arrive. I was relieved to see them and while I tried to decide whom to run to, they both approached me.

Professor Matthews was the first to ask how I was feeling, but Amanda was only two words behind.

"Nervous, very nervous. How many people are expected to be here?"

"Including cameramen, sound crew and the reporters, close to a hundred. This press conference will be much smaller than the others."

"How many others are there?" Amanda asked.

"I'm sorry, Professor Matthews, this is my best friend Amanda. She's seeing Gary, who is in your class with me. Amanda, Professor Matthews." Although she was very familiar with him, this was their first official meet.

"There should be at least three. This one for sure, one more before Natalie goes to the conference assuming there is time, and at least one when she returns. They'll all be very similar and if she does as well today as she did last night she'll be a pro in no time. Looks like things are about to get started. Why don't you grab a seat in the front row? I'm sure your support will help our emerging star."

Amanda headed off and sat in the very center seat in the front, eagerly looking towards the stage. I turned to Professor Matthews when he told me to follow him and we made our way backstage. The professor wasn't very surprised when I told him that it was my first time in the back of the school's auditorium.

"This experience will be filled with a lot of firsts for you. You look fabulous by the way. The cameras will just eat you up."

"You don't look so bad yourself, Professor Matthews." I was surprised when I saw *his* face redden — was what I said too bold? I didn't think so; it was just a tiny, but true, compliment. He was dressed quite formally in a suit and tie, no jacket, and I had never seen him like that. The moment was awkward but quickly passed when we heard our names announced. We wished each other one last bit of luck and walked onstage.

The room was in complete silence until the minute sounds of cameras began to hum. Lights were flashing from every direction and I was blindly led to a seat on the right side of the podium. Professor Matthews was up first.

The questions he fielded seemed typical, if there ever was a typical question out of a reporter's mouth. Questions came quickly and every answer of his seemed satisfactory. My eyes finally adjusted to the cameras' incessant flashes and I was able to see Amanda's familiar smile. Just as I began to get comfortable, I heard Professor Matthews introduce and then call for me.

I stood and approached the podium, anxious to get the day over with, yet wanting to savor every minute of the entire experience.

As if I were on autopilot, I began answering the all-too-familiar questions that Professor Matthews had prepared me for the previous night. And then a reporter asked a question that I wasn't prepared for.

"Do you hope to be able to solve the murder of your parents after attending the Science in U conference?"

Chapter 9

It was the first time in a long time that I felt the blood drain from my head. The faces of the audience members morphed into those of my parents. All I could see were multiples of the two people I missed the most. The last memory I had of them was filled with spilled blood and vacant eyes, the smell of baking, then burning. Cookies and blood.

As the faces merged into the last day I had seen my parents alive, I felt sick and stepped back from the podium. I was suddenly a kid again, arriving home from my first day of second grade and feeling excited to tell my parents all about it. Each previous year my mother had met me at the bus stop at the end of our street, so when she wasn't there I began to worry.

As I got close to the house I saw that the front door was open and the breeze brought with it the smell of chocolate chip cookies. My worry ceased as I made my way into my home. When I reached the screen door I hollered in, but no one answered. The smell of cookies suddenly turned foul and I set my backpack down and took off my shoes. I called out again and in return heard nothing.

I walked slowly into the kitchen and abruptly froze. My mother was in the kitchen, lying awkwardly on the table. Something was sticking out of her back. The beeping sounds of the oven kept me from fainting after I saw all the blood.

Coming to some sort of senses, I grabbed the phone from the table and called my father. I heard a muffled ringing from deeper within the house. I dropped the phone and ran out the door, scared of whoever was still there. I never made the connection that it was my father's phone being left unanswered.

I didn't bother putting my shoes back on. I just ran as fast as I could to my neighbors'. I reached their door and started beating on it until Mr. Witt finally answered.

"My mother's dead and I don't know where my dad is. There's someone in the house, the cookies are burnt and I don't know how to turn off the oven…"

I wasn't finished talking but I had ran out of breath, and Mr. Witt took that pause to invite me inside. My legs were frozen so he carried me in. He set me down on the couch and called his wife in. He talked quietly to her for a brief moment and then turned to me. He asked if I'd mind explaining things to Mrs. Witt while he made me lemonade. I hoped that he was calling the police but couldn't be sure that he even believed me. This type of thing just didn't happen in this town; even at seven, I knew that.

I stared blankly at Mrs. Witt and then everything came flooding out. I told her about my school day, how my mother always met me when I got off the bus but how she hadn't that day. Minute details were exaggerated — a funny thing shock did to my thought process while I rushed over the worst details in my head.

When I finished talking, I completely shut down. I made a surreal promise to myself to only speak again to my father. Mrs. Witt probed and pried and seemed annoyed that I refused to answer her. She left me, turning the television to some cartoon and left the room to return shortly with her husband and her daughter, my future best friend.

"Natalie, honey, we can't get a hold of your daddy, but the police and ambulance are on their way. They'll need to talk to you about what you told us. We know it will be difficult for you so we'll be here when you need us."

Sarah Butland

Difficult? I just saw my mother's blood, a lot of it. Reliving the experience would be impossible, not difficult. But it wasn't as impossible as I'd hoped; the image repeated in my mind hundreds of times before the police officer came to see me. She sat beside me and told me how sorry she was that I had to see that horrible scene. Trying to comfort me, she told me that no one should ever have to see what I saw — as if I didn't already know.

The radio on her waistband came to life, calling her Officer Fraser, and she excused herself. When she returned, I thought I saw tears in her eyes. She sat on the chair across from me this time, so I knew what she had to say was even more difficult.

"Natalie, honey, I have more bad news for you that I've never had to tell a little girl before."

"Is it Daddy, did you find him?"

"We did, Natalie, but it's not good news."

Chapter 10

I was brought back to reality when a slamming door echoed throughout the empty auditorium. Only Brian and Amanda remained. Somehow during the memory I had been seated, the conference ended, and the room cleared.

"Natalie, I'm so sorry. I underestimated the ignorance of local reporters and never expected such a drastic question. If there's anything I can do for you, please just ask."

Amanda answered for me, "We'll need some time alone. Please explain our absence to both of our morning teachers. If we can't make it back in the afternoon, I'll call you." Brian nodded, then exited without another word. "Let's go back to my place, Nat, or did you want to change?"

"There's a change of clothes in my car. I'll get the car and meet you at your place." After seeing the surprised look on her face, I added, "I'll be fine. I could make the trip with my eyes closed...but I won't."

I walked to my car like a baby taking his first steps, slow and deliberate, taking one slow breath after another. When I reached the car I eyed my bag and sat in the driver's seat. Putting the keys in the ignition and then checking the rear-view mirror, I caught a glimpse of my pale face, but I looked more like my mother than myself. The tears began to fall.

I saw her putting on make-up, watching her from the bathroom door and taking everything in that I could. She didn't wear much: just lipstick a shade darker than her ruby lips and mascara to curl her long lashes. She always told me I was too beautiful for make-up but I didn't understand that; she told me I looked just like her. I didn't see the resemblance, though I yearned to.

She'd pull her curly light hair back in a ponytail while mine fell flat and straight.

All of my friends either looked much more like their mother or their father. People said I just looked like me and that was best. I supposed it was, and eventually learned to cherish the similarities in our personalities instead of dwelling on what lacked physically.

Minutes passed before I realized that someone was knocking on my car window. Amanda had decided that she was going to follow me back, but when she saw me crying she decided I couldn't safely drive myself. I quickly agreed, grabbed my bag and got into her car. We didn't say a word to each other until we arrived at her place.

"Coffee, tea, or my specialty?"

"What's your specialty?" I wasn't interested in playing games.

"Hot double chocolate with marshmallows and a bit of Bailey's. I always make it for Gary when he's had a bad day. He says it works."

"I guess it wouldn't hurt."

"Coming right up. The remote is right there if you just want to veg." As soon as she was out of sight, the shaky dam broke once more. I didn't try to hide my tears when she returned. She set the mug on the table beside me and curled up on the opposite side of the miniature couch.

"Today must have been hard for you. No one will blame you for ending the press conference early."

"That's not it. Reporters are savages and I'll have to face them all again. I don't know if I can take it another time but I need to go to the Science in U conference. This is my last chance for this great of an opportunity."

"I know. Maybe if you talk about how you're feeling more freely, you'll stop seeing the horrific image. Have you told the prof?"

"No, all he knows is that my parents died when I was young and that since then, I've lived with your family. I don't want people to sympathize with me and take pity on me. I got to where I am today with hard work and I'm not going to give up now. My classmates will always think he's playing favorites and that he looks at me differently. What happened to me then was difficult, but I'm dealing with it."

"You're not dealing with your parents' murder. You're trying to bury it, and you've tried to bury it since you've buried them. Have you even told Professor Matthews?" She didn't realize that only my father's body was buried. I didn't correct her and despite how softly Amanda stated everything, the barrier collapsed and the dam burst.

"I know you're right. I just don't know how to deal with this." I was too embarrassed to admit that I had never revealed my parents' murder to my professor.

"I don't have any miraculous advice to offer you but I think it's time that you try another method. Maybe by opening up and embracing your situation you will avoid being bombarded by the sadness. I do believe you decided to study forensic science because of what happened to your parents — not to solve their crime, but to help others in a similar situation. You know that you're not alone. Even though you feel like you are a lot of times, you're not.

"I can be understanding when you need me to but because it never happened to me, I can never fully comprehend how you feel."

"I wouldn't want you to."

"I know, but I think that it would help you to talk to people who do understand. When you return from the conference why don't you organize some sort of support group for people who are in a similar situation as yours? Don't object before you sleep on it. I really do think that you can handle it. Maybe once a week or month. Professor Matthews would probably help you, or at least use it as extra credits toward his class."

My tears stopped before Amanda's speech came to an end and I began to consider the plausibility of her suggestion. I would think about it and told her so; she seemed genuinely impressed.

The hot chocolate was delicious despite it now being cool, and I barely tasted the alcohol. After finishing the drink in silence, I made up my mind.

"We should get back. Can you drop me off at my car first so I won't inconvenience you anymore for today?"

"Not a bother at all. I hate my morning classes anyway. Let's go."

The conversation on the way over was light, which helped to convince both of us that I'd be fine driving.

The rest of the day passed as just a regular day, but the phone started ringing as soon as I opened the door to my place. It was Professor Matthews.

"Good, you're home. Turn on Channel Eleven and call me back." My media fiasco was on television for the first time — but not the last time.

"Local student Natalie Hartman has been chosen by Professor Brian Matthews, a teacher at the University of Katula, to attend the Science in U conference. Natalie will be the first student from our area chosen in twenty-five years. Earlier today, our correspondent Jack Russel was on location at the first of a series of press conferences with the student…"

The news then played select clips of the event; of course, the main one they showed was Jack asking about my parents. I was amazed that the tears did not return, but what I did feel was an intense anger toward the reporter. I understood that he was just doing his job, but he was incredibly tactless. He had done his research but failed to realize he would be asking a human being the questions he had prepared.

My phone began ringing, but it took me a minute to decide whether or not to answer it. By the time I made my decision the ringing had stopped, but not for long. I answered the next call on the first ring.

Chapter 11

It was Amanda.

"Did you just call? Really, well, it must have been Professor Matthews, even though he told me to call him."

"Anyway, I just caught the tail end of the news. You looked fabulous!"

"Then you didn't see me collapse. Why didn't you tell me that I fainted and fell on my ass? Oh, never mind, the damage is done and it was clearly Jack's fault. I never want to see that man again."

"I've never heard you so angry, Natalie. Would you like some company?"

"Nah, it's still just my initial reaction. I'll get over it. Hang on for a sec, I have a beep," I clicked over and answered.

"Just checking up. When you didn't call I started to get worried."

My face flushed again as I pictured Professor Matthews in his stoic stance, worrying about me. I wondered if his normally slicked-back mane of fox-red hair was finally out of place. "Oh, sorry, no, I'm just on the other line with Amanda. You met her at the press conference. Can I call you back?" I clicked back over to Amanda and asked her if she had had a chance to talk to her professors about the trip.

"Actually, the profs I'm concerned with are my morning classes. I'll ask tomorrow and let you know. Gary just got home, so I'll let you go. Call if you need anything."

"I will, thank you again, Amanda. I'll talk to you tomorrow." Before I could call Brian back the phone rang again. "My, you're impatient. Couldn't wait for me to call back?"

Click. Amanda must have called back by accident, I thought, as I dialed Brian. He picked up on the second ring.

"Natalie? Good, how are you feeling? I understand seeing the news story may have been difficult. I didn't realize that particular reporter was from Channel Eleven."

"Oh, it's not your fault. I just hope that all press conferences will not result in my passing out on camera."

"I will call the station in the morning and have them pull Mr. Russel off the story."

"You can do that?"

"With your help, yes. As long as we can convince the station that he's a nuisance — which won't be a problem — they have to respect our wishes. Although this won't stop another reporter from picking up where he left off, it will force them to consider how they get their story."

Calming myself down, I took the professional approach. "Let me think about it. I have to consider the reporter in all this. He was just doing his job."

"Well, just let me know tomorrow during first class so that we can start the process before the next press conference. Have you given any thought to whom you're bringing with you?"

"Still thinking about it."

"I don't mean to rush your decision but the organizers need to know by Thursday to ensure flight availability."

"I know, I'm trying. I should know tomorrow. Actually, would you have any sway with Mr. Swan or Madame Gilles? Amanda wants to come and I can't think of anyone else I'd rather have with me. The problem is that both of those teachers are giving major tests the week of the conference and they are pretty set in their ways. If you can get them to let her take the tests a week early, everything will be set."

He promised to try speaking with Amanda's professors, but couldn't guarantee results. I crossed my fingers and went to bed. When I awoke I was drenched in sweat, though the apartment was cool from the autumn air blowing through the open windows. If I'd had a bad dream I couldn't remember it, and I was thankful for that small miracle.

I showered, dressed, and began to look for my hairbrush when I suddenly remembered that it was missing. Everything suspicious from the last few days came flooding back, and paranoia began to take over. I tried not to let it as I painfully finished combing through the knots in my shoulder-length wavy locks, but my mind was in turmoil.

It seemed that everyone at school had watched my public stumble, but they were surprisingly sympathetic about it. No one made an incredibly huge deal about it, for which I was grateful.

Professor Matthews came to see me in my first class, and as I walked out of the classroom to meet him I could almost feel my classmates glare at me. Jealousy was getting the better of a lot of my classmates, but I tried not to let it bother me. Between being hated and feeling completely paranoid, I was still churning with excitement.

"I wanted to give you your plane ticket as soon as it arrived and I wanted to tell you about my conversation with Amanda's teachers. I regret to inform you that they will not move her tests. Amanda won't be able to go with you if she plans to keep those credits."

I was devastated and speechless. My head spun with empty possibilities; Gary and Brian were among them. I just couldn't imagine sharing a hotel room with either man.

"The organizers bought an extra ticket for your guest anyway and it's for the morning of the seventeenth so you can have a good night's sleep before the class in the morning. The ticket for your guest will be held for further use, in case you think of someone else to take. The trip won't be as much fun for you if you go alone, but if you do you'll have plenty of study and free time. It won't be so bad. I'm sure you'll meet some friends there, too.

"The hotel room is booked with one queen size bed. The hotel ran out of rooms with two beds but if you decide on a guest, ask for one when you get there and hopefully they'll have one available."

"Are you implying that I need more study time?" The sarcasm was there, but not entirely evident; I just wasn't concerned with putting in the effort it required.

"Not at all, Natalie, just trying to look at the positive side of the situation. You shouldn't get down because you might go alone. You'll learn much more when you have a chance to absorb the information. And I'm sure you'll be able to charm your way to dinner with some of the other scientists. If you have that opportunity you wouldn't want to leave a friend to eat by him or herself."

Realizing I was holding him up and missing more class than I wanted to, I said, "Well, I better get back to class. Thank you for the ticket."

When I re-entered the class, the room was silent, but the students' eyes were directed towards their desks. The teacher whispered the reading assignment to me and I sat and took out my book. Just as I found the right page, class was dismissed.

Amanda was waiting for me when I exited the classroom and she wore a look of disappointment, a look very similar to how I felt. I asked if she had heard the news.

"I have, and I'm sorry. I just can't risk the credits but I'm sure you'll find someone to go. If not, you'll be fine going alone. I'd drop the classes but I think I've finally decided I want to teach, and I need these credits for that."

"Congrats! You'll be a fantastic teacher, Amanda. I know it's asking a lot of you to miss out on your classes. I just wanted my first trip to Disney World to be with someone special. I better get going, though. I don't want to miss any more classes than necessary. You doing anything tonight? I was thinking we could finally go out to celebrate, as the next couple of days are going to be pretty full."

"Tonight will be great. I'll call you at six and we'll set the game plan then." She may have said something else as I walked away but if she did, I didn't hear it. The corner I went around blocked my sight of her as well. I jogged to my next class, and although I was the last to take my seat I still arrived before the professor.

Six o'clock in the evening came before I knew it, but Amanda didn't call. I waited until quarter after six to call her. When there was no answer I called her cell, and she greeted me with an apology for not calling. Apparently she was out looking for Gary and wouldn't be able to hang out after all. I offered to help her, but she said she needed to look for him on her own. She couldn't explain why right then but promised to later, so I wished her luck.

Feeling disappointed at having been stood up, I went in search of dessert, which, for a lonely university student, was often eaten before or instead of supper. I found half a carton of Rocky Road, sat down at the kitchen table, and pulled out some schoolwork. Before long, the ice cream was gone and I was still staring at a blank page.

Professor Matthews had suggested that I begin preparing notes for the next press conference, as well as start thinking about the essay I would be required to write when I returned from Florida. I couldn't do much to prepare for the press conference because it had been confirmed that my next one would be when I returned. There just wasn't enough time to fit in another one before I left, so the press would make up for it afterwards.

Although focusing on something else seemed easy enough, I couldn't get Amanda's suggestions out of my head. I hadn't told her yet but I had already decided that organizing a support group for people who were close to a murder victim was an excellent idea; I was only disappointed that I couldn't start on the project immediately. I was thrilled and wanted to begin searching for people who could benefit from the group, but would have to hold off until my return from the conference. Amanda's second idea of inviting Gary to go with me wasn't far behind.

I packed up my things and went to bed. I woke with a startle, only minutes before my alarm was scheduled to sound, but I struggled to remember my dream. I came up with fragments, but those pieces were enough.

Chapter 12

I had dreamt that I was at Disney World with my parents. We were running to the next ride and I was a few feet ahead of them. When I reached the end of the line for the ride, I looked behind me for my parents but didn't see them. I began feeling anxious and turned back to the line of people, only to see that they had vanished.

Instead, I was standing at the entrance to the Arm Farm, and despite my restraint, I was moving towards the 'D' tree. Unfortunately, as dreams tend to go, this was no longer an ordinary tree but the one with knives as branches that I had dreamt about before.

I awoke drenched in perspiration and decided to call Amanda while I drew a bath. I would have to revert to visiting my special world again.

I was about to hang up when Amanda answered. I apologized for waking her and rambled on about my nightmare so quickly and without pause that I almost didn't realize she was snoring. I hung up, grabbed my nearest childhood stuffed animal, and let the loneliness invade my being.

I set my stuffed cat on the toilet seat as I slipped into the bath and tried to forget the dream, while struggling to avoid slipping into my usual escape.

Shivers woke me from my trance; I couldn't decide if they were the result of the cooling water or my resurfacing fears. It did not matter; wrapping myself in a towel seemed to calm the shakes, and the distraction of preparing for class made me forget about them entirely.

When I was fully dressed with keys and doorknob in hand, the phone rang. Not one to miss a call, I dropped my keys on the counter and replaced the doorknob with the cordless phone.

"Hello."

"Oh, I'm glad I caught you. I need you to call me right after class and tell me if Gary was there."

"Did he not come home?" She didn't mention my earlier phone call that had woken her up, so I didn't either.

"He didn't come home or call, email, or text me...this isn't like him. I'm worried."

"I'm so sorry, I'm sure it's nothing. I gotta run but I'll call the minute I can."

Gary was in class; he was hard to miss, as he occupied the seat next to me, but Brian began his lecture before I could question him. When class finished, Brian asked to speak with me and I forgot about calling Amanda. It wasn't until my phone rang on my way home at the end of the day that I realized I had let my friend down.

Hoping it was Amanda calling, I answered with a rushed apology, but the call was another hang-up. I was so annoyed that I resolved to have my number changed, but would only do so after I informed my friend that I had seen her boyfriend in class. Gary answered the phone.

"Oh, you're home. Is Amanda there?"

"No, but I expect her home any time now. Are you coming over?"

"She just asked me to call her about something so I wasn't really planning on coming."

"I can take a message —"

"No, that's alright, I'll just call her cell."

"She actually left that here. I'm looking at it right now, which is weird because that girl never goes anywhere without it. Do you think I should be worried?"

I wished I had said, "Like she was worried about you when you went missing last night?" Instead, I told him he didn't need to worry, then hung up and turned my car around in the first parking lot I saw. I needed to find Amanda and I knew right where to start looking. I just needed to get there before Gary figured out what I was up to.

I parked illegally and took the library stairs two at a time, reaching the reference section in record time. It was deserted. I asked the librarian if she had seen Amanda recently, to which she replied that she hadn't seen her in days. Too many weird things were happening and I could not wait for them all to end.

I took my time going back down the library stairs and debated where to check for Amanda next. Deciding on the less obvious option, I turned my car towards the pier and noticed that Gary's car wasn't far behind. Not knowing whether to elude him or let him help me, I realized Amanda would just keep running if she saw him. This was a sole mission, so I parked my car in the pier's crowded parking lot and ran into the arcade.

My attempt to lose Gary wouldn't be so obvious because the arcade was a favorite hideout for Amanda, but I just knew she wouldn't be there today. When I was confident I had lost my tail, I escaped to the wharf and ran.

I wanted to shout when I saw Amanda sitting on the hood of her car at the edge of the cliff but thought the silent approach would be safer. I sat beside her and watched the waves crashing to the shore and birds swooping for food until she broke the silence with a startling question.

"Are you seeing Gary again?"

"What? No! Why do you ask?"

"I think he's cheating on me and you didn't call after class."

"I know, I'm sorry. He was there but I didn't have a chance to talk to him, and then Professor Matthews told me more about my trip. In the excitement I forgot all about calling you. Gary and I are over, Amanda, and he's in love with you."

"I know," she said without confidence. "Don't be sorry, I shouldn't be asking so much of you when you're getting ready for the trip of a lifetime. I just can't imagine what I'm going to do without you."

"You'll be fine...it's only a week. I'll be back before you even realize I've left. But what's this about Gary cheating?"

The story was simple but it scared both of us enough that neither of us knew what to do. Amanda, convinced she knew the signs from watching her parents go through infidelity, felt betrayed, alone, and confused. I was speechless because I, too, was now convinced that Gary was cheating but didn't want Amanda to know I thought so. He was being too weird, too nonchalant when she asked where he had been, and disappeared far too often for it to be nothing. "I don't believe that, not of Gary. When would he have the time — no, *why* would he?"

Amanda kept repeating the words "I don't know" until I interrupted with "Did you ask him?" Anyone in Amanda's position wouldn't consider such a simple thing an option.

"What would I say?"

"The truth. You have no reason to lie and even less reason to hide your feelings. I've never known him to lie, especially to you. Stay at my place tonight and consider it. Call Gary to tell him you're all right — he's worried, you know. We'll talk again in the morning after a good night's sleep."

"Aren't you too busy?"

"Not so busy that I can't help a friend. My car is parked at the arcade, do you mind driving me back?" I was about to tell her that Gary would probably be waiting there too, but at the last minute, decided to keep silent. My friend would refuse my request for a drive if I did, and I wasn't in the mood to waste the time needed to walk back.

When Amanda saw Gary's car, she slowed to a stop and suggested I could walk the rest of the way. Declining her offer, I stayed put as we watched Gary leave his car and jog to Amanda's. Tempted to let Gary take my place, I decided it was safer to stay put, though I wasn't clear who it was safer for: Amanda, or Gary.

Chapter 13

Amanda rolled down her window and said, "I'm spending the night at Natalie's. I'll be back tomorrow." Without even a glance in Gary's direction, she started to roll up her window, stopping only to take her cell phone from Gary's outreached hand, and continued the drive to my car, leaving Gary standing in the middle of the road and us giggling at his embarrassment.

"Men." we said in unison and promised to follow each other back to my place.

We arrived to discover fifteen messages on my machine: thirteen from Gary and two from Professor Matthews. The professor said he needed to have the name of my guest by tomorrow. I was still not any closer to knowing who that would be. It was times such as this that I missed my parents the most, not only for the chance to take one of them with me but because I was without a sibling to turn to. Then I listened to Gary's messages again and I was more confused than ever.

Each message was a bit more panicked than the last — each, of course, in search of Amanda. I didn't know what to say in the situation and Amanda constantly wiped away fresh tears as we listened to the messages together.

"How could I suspect him of cheating? He cares so much for me," my friend mumbled.

The ringing phone saved me from having to respond to her; it was Gary again. He wanted to talk to his girlfriend, so I handed Amanda the phone. I left the house to pick up some hot chocolate so she could make us her specialty and forget her troubles, if only for a moment.

During the walk to the store, I tried to decide whether Amanda would even still want me to invite Gary. Although it would be an uncomfortable situation, he was my last option and I knew that Amanda and I could last through anything. I just didn't want to doubt the strength of their relationship.

Returning to an empty apartment, I didn't think it was safe to assume Amanda went home so I called her cell phone. I heard it ringing in my bedroom and saw her head poking slightly out of a jumble of blankets. She needed her rest, so I made my own hot chocolate, minus the Bailey's, though it was not nearly as good as Amanda's specialty would have been.

When my phone rang I was quick to pick it up and even faster to hope that it was Gary. It was Professor Matthews.

"I'm sorry for calling again," he started, "I just wanted to make sure you got my messages."

"I did and I've been thinking long and hard. I'm considering inviting Gary Cross but I have to think over a few things first."

"If it helps you decide, I think he would be an excellent choice. Both you and he would benefit greatly."

"Oh, that I know, but if I take him, it affects more than just the two of us. I have to think about it, Professor, but I will call you tomorrow morning." Amanda was standing behind me and heard my every word.

"I'm sorry. I just realized you were here. I tried to be quiet and let you sleep."

Her eyes were glazed over. At first she looked as if she had been crying, but then I realized, thankfully, that she was simply groggy. "The break might be good for both of us. I don't mind if you want to take Gary. It was my suggestion, remember?"

"But that was before..."

"Before I became obsessed, hysterical, and suspicious? I know, but the only thing I'm sure of right now is how good some space could be for both of us. Go and call him so you can put your mind at ease."

"Thank you for being such a great friend. Someday I hope to figure out how to make this up to you."

"No need, I'll just enjoy the break, the time alone."

I gave Amanda a quick hug and called Gary.

"Hi, Nat. Amanda's not here."

"Actually, she's still here. I called to speak with you."

"Oh?"

"I have an extra ticket to Florida and thought you might want to join me..." There was a long pause and I thought we had been disconnected. "Gary?"

"Yeah, sorry, I just...what do I say? Are you serious? I'd love to!"

"You wouldn't be attending the workshops or anything but you'd sure be a great help and support at the end of my day."

"Does Amanda mind?" I sensed hesitation in his voice and pictured him pacing. He always paced while on the phone, faster when he was nervous.

"Nope, she has actually been encouraging me to ask you. We leave on the morning of the seventeenth and the workshops start early on the eighteenth. Can you be ready?"

"Of course! I'll pick you up and that way we'll only have to pay parking for one car," Gary offered.

"No, that'll just leave Amanda without a car. I'll come and get you."

"Sounds fair. I should run, though, there are a lot of things I should get done before we go. Wow! Nat, thanks again."

"No, thank *you,* Gary. We'll talk again soon."

A part of my mountain of stress was dissolving and I again had my best friend to thank, but when I realized that Gary hadn't even asked about her, I felt troubled.

She was so intelligent, yet was oblivious to so much. Still, I was becoming increasingly nervous of her attention to her parents' case. It happened years ago and the police now considered the case cold; they only reviewed it briefly when they had no other cases to solve, which wasn't often in Boston. The police had gotten no further with the case than they had at the time of the murders, but Natalie was determined and had much more time and reason to continue searching for answers.

But the answers could never *be found. I had been so careful. It was so seemingly random of a murder that the chances were slim, but I would need to keep a close eye on this future forensic scientist. Everyone knew she wouldn't become a professor like Matthews; she would be in the field solving crimes. I had to take precautions, but not yet — not when she was still oblivious to anything substantial. Being on her radar now wouldn't do any good; I would stay low for now but continue watching.*

***

I picked up the phone and excused myself from Amanda, then dialed Professor Matthews' number automatically. When a female voice said hello, I questioned my memory. "Hi, I'm looking for Professor Matthews."

"Just one second. Can I tell him who's calling?"

"Sure, it's Natalie Hartman, one of his students."

"Oh, Natalie! You're the student he selected for the conference. I've heard so much about you...oh, excuse me, I'm Brian's daughter, Sam. I'll go get him."

I never knew he had a daughter. I didn't know if I was speechless due to this new information or because a pang of jealousy rang through my chest, if just for a brief flash. I had never noticed a ring on Brian's finger, but I knew that a lot of men didn't like wearing jewelry. I couldn't believe how much time I was taking of Brian's when he could be spending time with his family. I was ashamed, first from my bout of jealousy and then for taking up so much of his time.

"Natalie?"

"Oh, sorry, I was caught up with watching a movie."

Stupid, stupid, I berated myself for not hearing him speak until then. "I decided to take Gary with me and already ran it by him. I also just wanted to let you know that I decided I don't want you to call the station about that reporter. I have to gain confidence, and he'll only help with that."

"Are you sure?"

"Positive. And, Professor Matthews, I'll just see you at school tomorrow. Enjoy your evening." I hung up before he could say another word and sat on my couch, exasperated by my new knowledge. Brian never mentioned a daughter or a wife to my classmates or me, and I found that very unlike him. I didn't know how I could face him the next day but knew that I must.

Amanda decided to face the music and go home, saying I had enough on my plate to not have to worry about her. Shortly after her departure there was a knock at my door. Knowing that Amanda was long gone, I tried to recall if I was expecting any other visitors and came up empty. Looking through my peephole, I saw a bouquet of flowers and opened the door.

"Delivery for Natalie Hartman."

"That's me," I said and took the assembly of beautiful blooms, realizing it was an actual plant and not a temporary remarkable sight. The sender couldn't have known me too well if he thought I could keep these alive. However, the flowers were my favorite color of orange, so the giver couldn't be that oblivious.

"They have been watered so they won't need it again for a few days." The delivery person's voice sounded familiar and his face also looked familiar, but I figured he just had a common look. I said thank you and closed the door. Setting the flowers in the center of the table, I sat down to admire them before taking out the card and reading it.

To a terrific young lady
on her way to the top.
Secret admirer

Chapter 14

A few words that said a lot. I was still concerned that my secret admirer was Gary but I knew he wouldn't fess up to sending the flowers, even if he had done so as a thank you for inviting him to Florida. I thought of Brian and Amanda next but decided that neither had a reason to hide their identity, so the secret admirer had to be someone else. Someone who knew I was going to the conference, which, at this point, included a lot of people. It had to be someone who knew my address. The puzzle was collecting more pieces and the ones that I already had weren't shaping into anything. I welcomed and despised receiving the new additions.

I didn't know if the camera was necessary, especially since she'd be gone in a few days, but I had to take every step possible. Continuing to break into her apartment would deem detrimental and I was more interested in seeing what she was doing than what her place looked like. Although I had been able to retrieve the pack of gum I had stupidly left behind, it would have contained too many fingerprints for my own good. She would never be able to lift a print from the bouquet's wrapping and I wore gloves to place the camera. She was getting too skilled too quickly.

Trying to get the mystery off my mind, I started packing and soon realized I didn't have very many pairs of shorts or t-shirts. Needing to go shopping, I called Amanda. "Hi, Gary, is Amanda home?"

"Yup, just a second."

"Hey girl, only a few days left. Gary's already packed, are you?"

"I have nothing to pack so will need to go shopping, you in?"

"Of course! Tomorrow night. I'll pick you up in the morning so we can leave right from school in the same car. That way we'll get it over with quickly. We'll get some fast food on the way."

My hand stayed rested on the phone after I hung up, but my mind raced back to the puzzle. It might be important to solve before I left town, but Amanda was right: the days were numbered. I thought of asking Gary and the professor to help, but decided they might just think I was being paranoid and would mock me. Maybe I would leave it alone until I got back. I went to bed while making a list in my head of the things I would need to get at the mall the next day, but before I completed the list my alarm went off.

I put myself together as much as possible, grabbed my purse and was putting on my shoes when the intercom sounded. I started to tell Amanda I'd be right down when I decided I wanted to see her reaction to the potted flowers, so I invited her up.

Amanda reacted in a way that told me she was as equally surprised by their presence as I was. "They're beautiful, Nat. Who are they from?" she asked as she reached for the card which I had mistakenly put back in its holder. "Ooo, a secret admirer. Any ideas?"

"None, I was hoping you had some. Ahh well...let's just get classes over with and then do some shopping."

We met at her car after school and I had my list in hand. Although it seemed excessively long I wanted to be sure I had everything I needed for the time away. We were on our way, filling the car with mindless chitchat, when I asked about Gary.

"We're working through things. I asked him about my suspicions and he comforted me with promises that I was a worrywart and that it was nothing more than my own paranoia."

Paranoia was certainly getting the best of *me* as I convinced myself that someone followed us to the mall and then inside the mall. I often looked behind my shoulder as Amanda was immersed in story telling, but I was unable to pinpoint the reason for my concern, especially when we were in her car. But if someone knew my habits and vehicle they would certainly know Amanda's, so being in her car wasn't much comfort.

The stores were filled with long-sleeved shirts and raincoats, so the summer clothing line was slim pickings. I decided to buy just a few items and shop for the rest in Florida. I wouldn't have much time to vacation and I would need professional clothes for the most part, anyway. I'd be OK and besides, I needed to get home and away from the prying eyes of delusions.

"Did you want to spend the night?"

"I can...are you sure nothing's wrong?"

"I'm sure. Why would something be wrong?" I knew Amanda realized how unsure I sounded. She wasn't a woman from whom I could keep a secret.

"All right, as long as you'll let me help you prepare for your trip instead of getting in the way."

"Well, we'll have to rent a movie to get some girl time in. Your visit can't be all business."

Instead of going back to her place for clothes, I bought some for her. After all, she had agreed to look after my cat while I was gone.

During her stay she was the one who noticed the video camera in the potted flowers. I was so embarrassed that I hadn't noticed it myself, but was too traumatized to do anything except cry and blubber to my friend about what was happening — or at least what I thought was happening.

Amanda hushed me while she donned a pair of gloves from my tool kit on the table and removed the camera from its hiding place. Without a word she put the camera in the back of my closet and then returned, whispering, "It might have audio and I'm sure we don't want whoever may be listening to hear all you have to tell me. What's going on, Natalie?"

"Oh, Amanda. Thank you," I whispered through tears and sobs. "I can't believe I've been so naïve. I really don't know where to start, or how this will end."

"Start at the beginning, as they always say."

"That's the thing, I don't know where it all began. None of this makes sense." I had a nagging and sinking feeling that the story went back even further than the gum and the secret admirer note left in my car, but I couldn't put my finger on why.

Amanda convinced me to go to the police in the morning with all the forensic evidence I had gathered. I almost regretted having accepted the invitation to Science in U because since that moment, everything seemed to be falling apart. Amanda told me not to be so crazy, but it was my time not to believe her.

Amanda called Gary to let him know where she was, but he didn't answer the phone. She left him a message explaining that she wouldn't be home until tomorrow afternoon because she had agreed to accompany me to the police station. In fact, she told me she had already decided to go with me whether I invited her or not.

I thought about not even going to bed that night because I knew I wouldn't be able to sleep, and if I did, my sleep would be filled with nightmares. But when Amanda suggested we pack it in, I didn't object and made my way to bed. As I lay staring at the ceiling, I concluded that no one I knew would ever put me through the trauma I was facing. The secret admirer had to be someone I didn't know; I wouldn't have the time to find out who it was before I left for the conference. Even with police help, the forensic testing would take weeks and I only had days. I drifted off from exhaustion with that terrifying thought filling my head.

I dreamt that I was in class taking notes on crime scene etiquette when Professor Matthews began showing pictures of crime scenes for us to discuss. When I looked up from my papers I couldn't believe my eyes. I was staring at photos of my parents' murder, and yet it couldn't be possible. My parents' case was still open and we were never able to see open case files in class. I raised my hand and began to ask a question, when I suddenly vomited.

Chapter 15

I awoke with a start, covered in sweat; my heart was racing and my breath was trying to catch up.

I spent the rest of the night in the tub replacing cold water with hot. My skin began to resemble an aged sundried tomato but I still delayed getting out of the tub. It was only when Amanda knocked timidly on the door that I stood and wrapped my robe around my shivering body. Before answering, I stood and watched the water drain below me, oblivious to the panic Amanda was experiencing.

"Nat, is that you?" Her voice was almost a whisper and I quickly realized why she sounded so terrified. It wasn't a need for the bathroom, but for the confirmation that I was safe. I answered back, saying I was fine and opened the door. Her face was, for once, paler than my own, and I hugged her as I recounted my dream until she was hugging me back.

Amanda showered while I gathered up the video camera and the other evidence I had found. When I explained to her about the nicotine gum, she realized my concern with Gary's inconsistencies and promised to grill him on it. However, we had bigger fish to fry today: I was able to find all the evidence except for the Nicorette and became concerned. I knew I had put the evidence together in two places; the camera was on its own but everything else I had found was in the same place. The gum was a key piece of evidence so it was my turn to go into panic mode.

Amanda was really worried when she emerged from the bathroom to find my house turned upside down.

Still squeezing her long curly hair with a towel, she asked what was wrong.

"The pack of gum is gone. I had it with everything else but it's simply not there now. Amanda, it's gone! I was going to give it to Gary but after all this other stuff began piling up I decided against it."

"It couldn't just disappear. Calm down, get some breakfast and I'll be out to help you find it in a minute."

"Amanda, you know me. I don't lose things. The gum isn't in the house."

"Who would have been here since you found it?"

"Just you and…just you inside." I found myself doubting my friend but couldn't believe she would put me through this. "Did you pick it up still thinking it was Gary's?" The question was out of my mouth before I knew it and I immediately regretted asking. Being such a great friend, she only responded with a shake of her head and continued getting ready.

Deciding I still had enough evidence for the police to investigate, we left in silence and arrived at the station.

"I can't believe you would ask me if I took the gum, but I also understand you're stressed right now so I'm going to let it go." I turned my head as Amanda spoke, but she continued to look straight ahead. I sensed a tear in her eye and a frog in her throat, but she wouldn't let me see or hear either. After all these years she was hell-bent on not letting me see her cry.

"I'm sorry, Amanda. I really just don't know what to think."

"I don't need excuses. Let's just forget it happened and get this case solved. Do you mind if I leave my contact information with the police in case they find something while you're gone?"

"Absolutely not. I would greatly appreciate that." I didn't want to voice my concern about being alone with Gary now. I felt I needed to but this just wasn't the right time. There would never be a right time to doubt my best friend's choice in boyfriends, and besides, the plane ticket had been transferred to Gary's name and he was already packed. There was no turning back, unless some definitive proof that he was the culprit came in before it was too late. "Let's go."

It had been years since I had been inside a police station and I wasn't taking it well now. Flashbacks from childhood started as soon as I passed through the door and the sight made my knees wobble. The layout was the same but everything looked smaller. When I was seven years old the desks looked huge, the pictures on the wall looked too far away, and then there were the handcuffs and the cells lining the walls. The police officer sitting with me those many years ago let me play with her badge, but it had given me no relief. Now things were the right size and I finally felt protected.

I quickly took a seat in the waiting area while Amanda explained our presence to the receptionist, who sat nodding and finally showed some concern on her face. She made a phone call as Amanda took the seat beside me and held my hand.

"Does she believe you?"

"Of course she does, sweetie." That statement both terrified and comforted me.

Only seconds passed and I counted each and every one of them as if they were the last of my life before an older policeman came to see us. "Natalie? My name is Detective Charles Brock but you can call me Charlie." I took his extended firm hand with one of my shaky ones and was tempted to use it to help me stand, but refused to appear weak. I stood on my own, picked up the bag of items sitting at my feet, and followed him into the office. Amanda followed close behind.

Charlie held open the door for us both and closed it behind himself as he invited us to sit down. He didn't speak again until he was sitting at his desk. "Mona has told me you are having some trouble with a secret admirer and needed our help. Now, we don't usually meddle with something like this but she said it's best if we speak with you and get the full story."

"I appreciate that. If you think it's nothing after hearing the story I'll forget the whole thing ever happened, but it's been ongoing and worries me." I explained everything I was aware of, from the gum being left in my car to not being able to find it to bring in as evidence. I didn't leave out a thing I felt was relevant as to why I was taking it as far as the police. Charlie didn't interrupt even once and Amanda only nodded her head. Telling the story was a lot off my chest, but now I sat looking at Charlie and waited for him to respond. So many scenarios and hypotheticals ran through my head for what seemed like hours of silence.

"I understand your concern, Natalie, and I'll certainly take on the investigation myself. Although at this point I won't be able to send anything for DNA testing, because the evidence we have so far is too circumstantial. I do believe I have some people to question. I hate to say it, but I'll need to start with Gary because he was the last one to see your car before you found the gum and note." Amanda was taken aback but I expected the inquiry. Investigators always question the person known to be last on the scene. Amanda didn't verbally object so I told Charlie it would be OK to question Gary, but that he might have to wait for over a week to do so.

"It's best if I talk to him immediately since a lot of time has already passed and time only distorts memory. Is he not able to come in tomorrow?"

"We're actually leaving for Florida on Tuesday at noon, so he won't have much time and I really don't want him upset with me before we go."

"Isn't Gary Amanda's boyfriend?"

Amanda offered, "Yes, he is but he's studying forensics, too, and…"

"That's why I recognize you. I saw your news conference the other night. Congratulations on your success at such a young age. Your parents would be so proud."

"Thank you, Detective. So you really think we have a case?" I didn't want to get into it, so I let his ignorance about my parents go as he obviously didn't watch the entire news conference.

"I hate to say it but, yes. If you hadn't found the video camera I would have had to say no, but thanks to Amanda noticing it, we do have something to investigate. Although, like I mentioned, we can't go as far as testing the DNA yet, I will send the secret admirer's notes for writing analysis and fingerprints while you're away. I won't be able to do much on Monday, especially without anyone to question, but should have some results when you get back." He paused before he asked, "Would you mind if I questioned your professor?"

That surprised me. "Why?"

"He seems to be very close to you, spending a lot of time with you lately. I thought maybe he would have seen something, anything that might help."

"I wouldn't feel very comfortable with you questioning him but I do want answers. I just ask that you wait until I leave town if you can."

"I can respect that. Natalie, I know this is going to be very uncomfortable for you but you must understand, especially because you study criminal sciences, that the best place to start is with the people closest to you."

"I do, I know." Standing to go on still-shaky knees, I thanked the detective for his time and left the evidence on his desk. "If I find the gum I'll let you know, but I really don't think I will."

"What about dusting your place for fingerprints? Would you be OK with that?"

"But why…?" Not wanting to think of the possibility that someone may have broken into my place but realizing it had to be said, I agreed that he could dust on Monday night and apologized for the mess that would be there.

The receptionist smiled at us on our way out, and although I didn't feel much like smiling I returned the courtesy. Other than that, I counted the tiles on the floor and used Amanda as my guide back to the car even though she could barely lift her head either. I found my voice and told my friend not to be worried about the police needing to question Gary. "They're not saying he did anything wrong. It's a matter of seeing if he remembers anyone hanging around when he dropped my car off."

Amanda started the car and pulled out of the parking lot before speaking. "Two years of seeing a man and you find out you barely know him…"

Chapter 16

"Amanda, that's not true. We're not accusing Gary of anything…"

"No, you're too busy accusing me!"

"Amanda! Don't be like this, please. You're the only person I can talk to and I'm sorry I asked if you took the gum. It's just…"

"I know, I'm sorry, too. I'm completely jealous, yet I wouldn't ever want to be in the same boat as you. A secret admirer is one thing, but an admirer who stalks is too creepy."

"I certainly need this trip more than ever now, but I also wonder if this would all be happening if I wasn't going." I whined, pleading for Amanda to justify my leaving so much behind.

"Natalie, you're still going. You're going to have fun, work hard, and learn lots. The trip will help you forget about the stalker and will make you think about this situation differently when you get back. It'll also give me the chance to think about things with Gary."

"Don't make any rash decisions based on this past week, Amanda. Let's wait and talk it out when I get back." By this time we were parked in my driveway and I didn't want to get out. I'd always had issues with being alone since the death of my parents, but had been coping with being by myself well until now. "Did you want to come in?"

"I really should get back to Gary. It's going to be hard to pretend nothing is happening with you. I'm sure it'll be just as hard when you're reviewing your work with him in Florida, knowing he's a suspect. I'll give you a call later, though."

I thanked Amanda for everything and got out of the car. I stood looking at the window of my home while Amanda accelerated slowly out of the driveway and out of sight. Taking a deep breath through chattering teeth — because of the circumstance and not the rain — I picked my keys out of my purse and went inside. Quickly closing the door behind me, I double-locked it for the first time since I had moved in. I looked around, going from room to room to make sure all windows were closed and locked and that I was alone. I wasn't up for a bath again and knew I had lots to do before the trip, so I got busy organizing my new binder just the way I liked it. Deciding to include some of my class notes in the binder, I went to my room for my backpack, but it wasn't where I always left it.

"Sonofabitch," I muttered, knowing full well I had left my backpack at the foot of my bed. Seeing the phone sitting idle on my nightstand and then noticing its voicemail indicator flashing, I ran to it. Except I didn't run as hard as I had planned and instead fell on my face. Without much sleep, I didn't have my usually stellar reflexes and I could only imagine the burns my carpet would leave on my skin.

Cursing, I turned to see my backpack lying as if it had fallen off the edge of my bed. I kicked it for good measure, but now had the voicemail to worry about.

"Could be nothing," I whispered as I dialed. "Probably just Gary looking for Amanda." After struggling to punch in my voicemail password correctly, I listened to a familiar voice — but not that of Gary. Concentrating on placing the voice, I had to listen to the message again because the words were a jumbled mess. The second time around I realized very quickly that it was just Professor Matthews asking me to call him, which I did right away.

"Natalie, thanks for calling back...just one second," I heard him close a door and then search through papers before he started again. "Sorry, I'm here, I was just getting some details...ah, here it is." He went on to give me all the times and places for the Science in U workshops. I tuned him out and went back to worrying about my admirer. I needed this time away more than I had imagined. "Natalie?"

"Oh, sorry, just a lot on my mind."

"You must be excited and I'm boring you. How about I drop this itinerary off to you tomorrow morning?"

"Sounds good, I'll talk to you then." I disconnected the line long after I disconnected from the conversation. I suddenly realized that Whiskers wasn't home and I was concerned; he was always inside when it was raining. I stood looking at the cat door that my landlord had let me install in the back door, and pondered a lot more than the whereabouts of my cat. I saw the cat door's flap make its slow way inside but it wasn't my cat coming in — it was a hand holding a stuffed animal. As soon as I came to my senses and realized there had to be a person behind the hand, I ran to the door and swung it open.

The stuffed animal dropped to the floor and a human figure jumped clumsily from my balcony to the ground and out of sight before my eyes could adjust to the night. The baggy pants and bulky jacket in the unseasonably warm weather told me the outfit was a disguise — and a good one, too, as I couldn't even distinguish gender. "So much for being a good CSI."

I immediately ripped the stuffed animal apart, looking for a video camera or recorder and when I found nothing, I was pissed off. My knees buckled and I fell to the floor as I realized the stuffed animal was new evidence in addition to the video camera — and I had just destroyed it. Because of my frustration, only stuffing, a collar, and eyes remained. It wasn't the least bit adorable but could have been once, in a different situation, maybe. A *completely* different situation.

I had to stop taking such large risks. She wasn't a stupid girl, and I killed my ankle with the jump I took just in time to escape being seen. I could only hope that my simple disguise was enough to confuse her. Next time we would be this close to each other, we would be on a plane together on our way to Florida. I had a lot to do to prepare and couldn't be caught beforehand.

Or better yet, I could convince someone else to go, someone who wouldn't ask questions but would follow instructions well. Yes, I had to stay behind, but Natalie needed to be followed and I knew the perfect, most naïve person for the job.

Chapter 17

Dialing Detective Brock's direct number printed on his business card, I reached his voicemail. I hesitated to leave a message but decided to ask that he call me; then I hung up and dialed the police station. When the receptionist answered, I calmly told her that I had a case opened with Detective Brock and that I needed to update him. She told me he was off for the night but suggested I leave a message and that he'd call back tomorrow. "I've left one already so I'll wait for his call." I hung up with a lump in my throat. I wasn't sure that this should wait until tomorrow but decided it had to.

Now wondering if it was best to sleep at my place or to rent a hotel room for the night, I called Amanda for advice. "Natalie?"

"Yeah, it's me. Something happened..."

"What? Are you OK?"

"I guess so, I just...I..." I went on to explain what had happened until I heard her gasp and say she'd be right over. "No, Amanda, that's not why I'm calling. I tried to get a hold of Detective Brock but he's off duty, so I just wondered if I should sleep here or go to a hotel."

"Hotel. Get your valuables and go to a hotel. You don't know what this creep will do to your apartment when you're gone, but it can't be worse than what he might do to you if you stayed. Get out quickly and make sure you're not being followed when you do. Call me when you get to the hotel but don't tell me where you are. I'll call your cell if I need you."

"You're right, I can't stay here. I'm really worried about Whiskers, though. He's still not back, and..."

"Worry about yourself for once. Call me when you get to the hotel." She hung up before I could say another word, so I put the phone down and began gathering some items for the night. I was happy to see Whiskers arrive just as I was overfilling his food and water dish. Knowing that he was back, I felt better leaving. Checking his litter box, I decided to move my barely-packed suitcase by Whiskers' own door so that he couldn't escape again. I grabbed my bag, took one final look around and left the apartment, triple-checking that the door was closed tightly and locked. I didn't think my admirer would be back tonight but I needed to be safe.

Looking behind me every second step, I kept my ears attuned to any unusual sounds but became convinced I wasn't being followed. Getting into my car, I quickly locked the doors and was on my way to the second-closest hotel to my place. I reasoned that this was would be better than staying at the closest and most obvious location, yet more convenient than going any further. I did have to be back at my apartment in the morning to meet Brian, and my gas tank was almost dry. I was too nervous to stop and fill up so I just drove.

I called Amanda just after getting myself safely into the hotel room and then changed into my pajamas and turned on the TV. The first channel was playing highlights of my press conference, so I changed it, finding a late-night movie to watch. Getting myself cozy under the blankets, I fell asleep with the TV still playing softly. I wasn't sure if it was screams from the TV or my own that woke me up. My nightmares were progressing just as my own life was becoming more terrifying, and I didn't like it. I needed sleep before my trip but I didn't think that was going to happen.

Turning the television off, I pulled the small blanket up to my chin and closed my eyes. I didn't sleep. I couldn't. I just lay there hoping for sleep, until morning finally arrived.

My cell phone rang as I was getting out of the shower and I guessed it was Amanda or Brian calling, so I decided to call them back after I brushed my hair. I realized suddenly that I was assuming again, dropped my towel, and ran for the phone. Missing it by just seconds, I waited to see if a voicemail would be left. When one wasn't, I checked the caller ID.

Chapter 18

'Caller Unknown.'

Helpful.

Staring at the phone a few minutes longer, I decided to go back to getting ready for the day.

Still nervous about the events that had brought me to the hotel, I called Amanda once I was dressed and asked her to meet me for breakfast. We only had a day left before my trip and I wanted to spend as much time with her as possible. She accepted the invitation, considering it our celebration. We met at First Meal of the Day, where we ate as much as we could. However, our plates still looked as if we lacked much interest in food consumption.

Amanda didn't mention my latest secret admirer incident until we sat back with our stomachs full, and I was thankful for the small reprieve. When the waiter returned, we asked him for coffee, knowing it would keep him at bay with the bill and our feelings of a guilty stay. If we had known how close we were to my stalker, we would have been out of there much faster.

She was so calm, pretending like it never happened. I pretended to be calm as I went over my errors and tried to determine where I went wrong. Hindsight always being cruel, I vowed to never get so close to my Natalie again. Unless she made it necessary.

My cell phone rang and I saw that Brian was calling. I excused myself and answered while remaining seated. Amanda got up to use the ladies room.

"Hi Brian...no, I just actually finished my breakfast. Amanda and I went out, so I'm not home yet."

"I'm not at your place, I was actually running late and calling to ask if you'd rather go out for lunch to discuss everything."

"Meet for lunch? I really shouldn't, I'm so full now and really want to save some spending money. Brian, I could never ask you to pay..."

"You didn't ask. I'll meet you at two at the Pinnacle." He hung up before I could object and the guilt set in just as Amanda came back to the table. The waiter was just behind her with our bill in hand. I offered to pay but Amanda insisted. Two great meals with two great people and right before my amazing trip; I was a lucky girl. I just wasn't convinced my luck was all good. Amanda tossed some cash on the table and I put in some of my own for the tip.

"Is there anything I can do for you today? Anything you need me to pick up or pack for you?"

Deciding to take advantage of her company, I replied, "Well, since you offered...I have tons to do. Of course I'll do the packing, but I would appreciate your company while I do it. I'm meeting Brian at two and would love to have it all done by then. Especially if I need to stay at the hotel again tonight."

"Natalie, I'd love to join you. Let's go." We left the restaurant arm in arm, clueless of the awkward looks some patrons directed towards us, one in particular giving a look I was lucky not to have seen. I was such a bag of mixed emotions, but knowing the law of attraction I wanted to project only the positive ones.

I was expecting to find my apartment exactly as I had left it, and save for a few things on the floor from Whiskers having gone stir crazy, it was. Amanda, like her true self, went directly to my sink and filled it with water to wash the few dishes I had left out.

"Amanda, please don't do that..."

"Ahh, I want to help and if this is all you'll let me do, then I'm going to do it. Go pack, pretend I'm not even here."

I escaped to my room, where I gathered all of my traveling clothes into my laundry basket, throwing hangers and non-essentials on my bed, then brought everything into the living room. I went to the back door for my suitcase and when I returned, I realized how clean my apartment was. Amanda could do amazing things in little time, and she proved it by cleaning everything except my bathroom and bedroom in the forty-five minutes it took me to gather my things for the trip. She grabbed and folded a shirt before I could say anything.

"Seriously, put that down. I have to do something for myself."

"I agree: you have to relax. Sit down and tell me how excited you are about this conference."

"How about we do the packing together and I'll tell you all about what I'm going to learn."

"As long as you don't go into the gory details. You know how I hate blood."

"Deal."

And that's what we did. Before we knew it my things were packed and it was only minutes away from 2:00 p.m. "Oh, I hate to run out on you but you can stay, as long as you promise not to clean anymore."

"I can't, I..." She didn't want to tell me how frightened she now was to stay alone in my place, but I knew immediately why she wasn't staying. It was just so hard to forget the horrible things that were happening. Even the good couldn't overcome the questions lurking everywhere! "I told Gary I'd make him dinner if he promised to be home and I have to go to the store first."

I freshened up and left right behind my friend. On autopilot again, I was halfway down the stairs before I realized I hadn't locked up. Why did I have to be so careful now with so much else going on? I returned and locked up tight after taking a quick peek inside to ensure that no one had gotten in and that Whiskers was still there.

Barely fashionably late, I saw Brian as soon as I entered the restaurant and caught up to him just as he was taking a seat. "Sorry I'm late, I was packing and lost track of time."

"Understandable. Just in time to order your drink." The waiter approached and took our order for a Pepsi and strawberry daiquiri, both without alcohol. He returned with our drinks within minutes, giving us little time to review the menu. We asked for a few minutes to decide, and while Brian looked quite perplexed over what to eat I pondered whether to tell him of my incident. When the waiter returned with notepad and pencil in hand, I casually yet quickly gave him my order. Brian ordered with more confidence than I had. When we were alone, I took a deep breath and...

"Thanks for meeting me. I have all the information you will need for your trip. I asked for a table for four so we could spread out and review anything in full if you wanted."

...let it out slowly.

"I appreciate you meeting me again, Professor Matthews. I keep thinking of how much work this has been for you and I wish that you were going to the conference too. I asked before but we were interrupted — you have gone, right?"

He explained that he had gone to Science in U when he was my age. I felt a bit ashamed for him but proud for me that I was surer of what I wanted to do and who I was than he had been at that time. Unlike me, Brian had never known what he wanted to do and when any opportunity gave him some insight, he jumped on it. A professor of his biology class was the one who recommended he study forensics, based on the topic Brian always chose for his essays.

Brian told me that as a child he once tagged along with his parents on a mountain climbing trip that was for adults. He picked everything up so quickly that no one seemed to mind. Brian said he had experimented with so much as a kid, taking a journey of rocky roads to find himself. When he came back from Science in U, he finally knew what he was meant to do; it just wasn't the direction that his biology teacher had predicted: "He had thought I'd go out in the field, not stay at the university to teach."

After we made our way through the wonderfully simple meal, the waiter came back to offer dessert. I declined because I was full and knew I had to work on a paper that was due on Monday. Even though I declined dessert I was hesitant to leave because I knew it meant I'd have to be alone. When we finally went our separate ways, I quickly made the decision to gather my schoolwork and a change of clothes from my place. I'd work on my assignment at the library — the one at the university was open late on weekends — and then I'd go back to the hotel.

I finished my paper in an almost completely deserted library and drove to the hotel, always keeping an eye on the happenings behind me. As far as I could tell, I wasn't being followed.

Chapter 19

Checking back into the hotel, I felt more relaxed than I had in a while. I vowed to keep the TV turned off and just try to sleep. Knowing I'd be too excited for restful sleep the next night and that I'd get up early, I hoped to rest for ten hours, if not more.

Sleep came a lot faster than I thought possible and I didn't wake up until my alarm sounded. Feeling less groggy than the day before, I got ready, checked out of the hotel, and went off to school. Funny thing was, I never even once noticed the red van following behind me. I felt more confident than I should have.

With everything in place and time to spare, I decided to follow Natalie to class. Sensing her increased carelessness for security, I was more relaxed but still careful. She made it to class and I stopped to let her cross the street to the campus. She waved at me and had a small smile on her face. I knew she recognized me and yet never thought twice about seeing me.

I handed in my paper and attended classes as if I weren't going away the next morning, but my mind was not on the present. I was already wondering what I'd be learning at the conference, thinking about the questions I wanted to prepare, and at the same time, thinking of my stalker. Although I felt secure knowing I'd be far away from home the next day, I still had to safely embark the plane. Even then, the adventure would just be starting in a whole new way.

After classes I finally filled up my gas tank and took the forty-five minute drive to my parents' graves. Supper could wait. I grabbed my sweater, locked the car, and made the slow walk to the matching headstones. My aunt, my mother's sister, had helped me pick them out and I was still thankful for her help. We weren't close; she had even decided not to adopt me when it all happened because she just wasn't a kid person. She had never married and was always traveling, but she'd done the best she could with me at the time.

Amanda wanted to come with me today, but I knew I needed to be alone. Despite my nerves, I couldn't stop living because some psycho had it in for me.

I talked to both my parents even though I knew that what remained of my father's body was no longer him and that my mother's casket was empty.

"It's me, Mom and Dad. I had to visit before I left because I wanted to tell you how excited I am. I'm going to the Science in U conference. You know, the one I've been telling you about for years. I know you would be proud. I also know you would be telling me to enjoy myself and follow my heart, but not to worry about solving your murder. Problem is, my heart is telling me I need to.

"I'm not studying forensic science just for you. It just helped me find my direction and I need to pay you back. My stomach has to stop turning at the smell of chocolate chip cookies. I'll be back in a few days and will tell you all about it. I miss you." At that, a tear fell as I looked around the empty cemetery. Standing for another moment, I took a deep breath, wiped my tears, and then turned to make the trek back to my car.

She looked right at me and didn't see me, thank goodness, or she would have suspected me right away. I hated cemeteries and should have sent my lackey on this task but couldn't risk her bumping into "Dana" so soon. It was weird to

Sarah Butland

think that but I found being there extremely creepy having done what I did. I crouched behind a headstone of some "Ethel Black" who lived from 1929 – 2003. I didn't much care. I was on a job and had to be careful. Natalie was consuming my life in a way I had never wanted her to, but I had a lot riding on the fact that her parents' case was unsolved. Obviously, my whole world would change drastically if there were any hint of my being a part of the murder.

I stayed put until her car was out of sight and then I took the slow way home, not concerning myself with the need to see her again that night.

The drive back was hard, but I knew I had to control my emotions as I had been practicing since the age of seven. I only had a couple of hours left to say my farewells, eat, and make sure I was ready because there wouldn't be time to do much in the morning. I had already decided to stay the night at my place; it would be more convenient to leave from there. I considered asking Amanda to stay with me but knew she'd want her last night with Gary for a few days to be special, so I forced myself to be brave. With all windows and doors locked and the police already looking into my case, I knew I'd be safe.

I opened my door and immediately looked for the phone to check for voicemail. I hadn't heard back from the police detective and was concerned. There was only one message, from Detective Brock.

"Natalie, sorry for not getting back to you sooner, I just got in, I'm working the night shift this week. When you get home, no matter the time, please give me a call. I hope everything is all right and that nothing else unusual has happened. My number is..."

I copied down the direct number from the voicemail instead of taking out the detective's card. He answered on the first ring. "Detective Brock speaking."

"Charlie, thank goodness I caught you. It's Natalie Hartman. I needed to catch you before I left. Something happened Saturday night."

"Are you OK? I'm on my way over to check for prints. Did you find the gum?"

"I'm fine, I just destroyed some more evidence, that's all. I had a special delivery again, this time on my back balcony — the platform on the fire escape. Someone delivered a stuffed animal through my cat's door in the back entrance. I freaked. Instead of preserving the evidence, I ripped it up in case there was a camera inside. I looked out but the person was too far away. All I saw was a hooded raincoat."

"Are you home now? I'm pulling into the parking lot right now, can you buzz me in?"

"Of course, I'm here. I should have remembered you were coming tonight. Wow, I might not be a good CSI after all."

"Don't say that. It's always different when you're the victim."

As I hung up the phone, the detective's last words echoed in my mind.

I'm the victim.

I'm a victim.

Why was all this happening? Why now? I was too good to have a stalker. Too innocent to be a victim. But that's what all victims said and how they all felt. Victims didn't ask to be victimized, nor did they do anything to deserve it. If I could just get my head back on my shoulders, this guy would have picked the wrong person to mess with. But I wouldn't feel like myself for another week or so.

The press conferences would take up much of the week after I returned, but I had to make time for my own case. Right now it was higher priority than even my parents' case — and that was saying something.

My doorbell rang as I was on my way to the fridge, startling me before I came to my senses and realized that it was the detective. As a precaution, I looked through my peephole to confirm that it was Charlie. When I saw that it was, I let him in quickly, locking the door behind him and his partner.

"Natalie, this is my partner, Detective Lincoln. I updated him on your case already. Can you tell us where the perpetrator was standing?"

"I'll show you." I took them to the back door and opened it, explaining and pointing to the important pieces of the story as I did.

Detective Lincoln opened his fingerprinting kit and began dusting. He promised he'd clean up after he was done, but like most cops, I had come to find out, he left a mess behind. I chalked it up to his being a man. I didn't mind; there wasn't much left to do for the trip and having a mess to clean up distracted me — but only a little.

Gary called while the detectives were there, so I promised to call him back when they left. He sounded curious about who I was seeing right before my big trip but refrained from asking, and for that I was thankful. When I returned Gary's call, Amanda answered and asked if everything was OK. I told her that it was and apologized for not being able to chat long.

"I know. You need your sleep. Gary was just waiting for you to call and then we'll be turning in, too. I'll put him on, just a sec."

"Natalie, thanks for calling back. I'm sorry for calling when you had people over. So what's the plan for tomorrow?"

"Let me double check our flight time," I said as I retrieved the tickets from my wallet, although I must have already looked at them a dozen times. "OK, the flight leaves at one in the afternoon and we need to be there at least an hour early to get past security. Would eight in the morning be too early? That'd give us time for a quick breakfast and still be there plenty early."

"Just what I was thinking. I have everything packed so I'll be waiting outside for you. That way you won't have to ring the doorbell, because Amanda's not sure if she'll be up."

"See you then, go get some sleep. And, Gary...thanks again."

"My pleasure, sleep well."

I felt more alone than usual once I put the phone on its charger and the plane tickets back in my wallet. I decided the only cure was sleep so I retired to bed. I slept better than expected and dreamt some satisfactory dreams about my parents. I actually awoke with a smile and realized it was the day that I was leaving almost everything behind for a few days — unless the problem was Gary. I was looking forward to the trip but hadn't had time before leaving to realize just how excited I was. This conference was bigger than any trip that full scholarship university students are sent on — and *I* had been chosen to go!

I let out an excited scream as I realized I had daydreamt for too long and had only twenty minutes to pick up Gary. No time for triple-checking everything, so I was happy to have double-checked the night before. I jumped in the shower, and then dressed in yoga pants, a t-shirt and a light sweater that I had laid out the night before, and spent four minutes with Whiskers. I was good to go and had Gary and his luggage in my car only seven minutes after 8:00 a.m. I wanted more time with Amanda, who was up but not going to the airport with us, but I had to be satisfied with a hug and a rushed goodbye. We were on our way. *I* was on my way!

The conversation on the drive to the airport was anything but awkward. Instead of us being silent and me letting nerves get the best of me, I liked that Gary filled the car with questions about my anticipation of the conference. Although he wanted to go, he had only heard of the conference a year before when enrolling in the forensics courses. I usually tried not to talk about myself, but I was too excited to follow that rule.

Chapter 20

Stopping at Kegan's Diner on the way to the airport, we both ordered a light meal, which Gary devoured and I picked at. The nerves in my stomach weren't allowing much to go down easily. Gary paid and we left with plenty of time to wait at the airport. He offered to drive, but I admitted I needed the distraction, the routine.

I continued babbling on the way to the airport and found myself pulling into a parking spot in no time. I was so nervous that I couldn't even remember what I had said in the car, but I was sure I had left out my stalker issues. At least I thought I was sure.

Like a gentleman, Gary offered to carry my luggage up the hill but when I declined, he excused himself for a minute and ran up ahead, leaving both his luggage and mine with me. I stood dumbfounded until I saw him coming down the hill with a luggage cart big enough for all of our things. The flattery he was giving me was worrisome and hard to ignore. I knew from Amanda and from my own brief time with Gary, that in the beginning of their relationship, he would open doors, buy flowers for no reason, and just overall be a gentleman. Apparently that didn't last for very long, and although he was still courteous, I think Amanda would have been shocked to see how he was acting with me. It was going to be a long trip.

We made it up the hill and even past security with no real issues. We didn't continue our conversation until we were seated and waiting to be called to board.

"I know she has class, but I expected Amanda to be here." I hadn't had a chance to ask her why she chose not to see us off, and I felt like an intruder asking Gary; I just felt I should.

"I know. I think she's just happy to see me out of her way, but what she told me was that she'd be better off going to classes today than waiting at the airport with us. I don't know what's wrong with her lately, do you?"

I had to play dumb; I couldn't be sure of what Amanda had confessed. I also didn't want to make a big deal out of it and have him dwell on it the whole time we were away. "I'm sure it's nothing, Gary. It's just her way of dealing with two important people in her life leaving her for a few days."

"But she was the one who suggested you take me."

The situation could have been more awkward than what it was already if it weren't for the announcement to board. Before we knew it, it was time for general boarding; we hadn't even noticed the call to board first class passengers and passengers needing extra assistance. I just prayed that I wouldn't be so distracted with my own personal problems during the conference.

Gary and I ceased our troubling conversation and made our way to our seats. I was fortunate to have the window seat in the middle of the plane, just a row away from the emergency row and far enough away from the engine for comfort. It wasn't until the moment that our carry-ons were put away and we were buckled in that Gary admitted that this would be his first flight ever. I realized he had been too nervous in the car to pay attention to my chatter, so I was safe even if I had mentioned a certain troublesome secret admirer — unless he was purposefully leading me astray. But I was sure I'd recognize a psycho, wouldn't I?

"Are you serious, Gary? Why didn't you tell me until now?"

"Couldn't be more serious. I was embarrassed, trying to be macho. I just realized it's not working very well. Any advice?" I dug into my purse and brought out two benzo's, asked him if he was allergic to anything, and when he said he wasn't, I handed him the medication. By the time the flight attendants finished their spiel Gary was knocked out. I was OK with that because I had some notes with me to review, and for almost three hours, I'd be safe and have time to think.

When the plane lifted, I saw the sense of security clearly on Nat's face. I was sitting a few rows in front of her, but it wasn't difficult to see her when I pretended to check my contact lenses. Just a simple mirror, and the reflection it provided delighted me. She had no idea, couldn't even fathom that I was on her tail. I produced a book from my carry-on and read some fiction while keeping my ears attuned to my beautiful prey and my head down, away from Gary's eyes.

I had begun thinking of Nat both as prey and sexy, believing that it made my task more exciting. I was undecided so far as to whether I'd let her know that she wasn't safe. I thought of following her to the bathroom or leaving something on her lap while she napped; the thoughts were invigorating, but acting on them would be a dead giveaway. I decided to stay quiet for now, only wanting to act if I was acted upon. I knew my "employer" would appreciate my keeping a low profile and I was already keeping my desire for Nat a secret. I hated keeping secrets, but they made this mission even more entertaining.

I forced myself to concentrate on the task at hand, as I'd have very little time other than the flight to work on my notes. I was able to read and absorb them all with time left to read a bit of the new Stephen King, both before Gary stirred and before our landing was announced. This was it: the first time I'd be landing in Orlando — and for such a great reason too.

I shook Gary, gently at first while calling his name, and when that didn't work, I shook him harder and finally resorted to slapping him. That finally did it.

"Wh-what? Oh...sorry. I've never taken pills that relaxed me that much. Is everything OK?"

"Everything is fine. You're a great travel companion. It's just that we're landing and I thought you'd want to experience at least one part of your first flight."

"Oh, thank you, you're right. Amanda likes the landing best, so I'm happy to be finally able to experience it."

The plane's wheels touched the ground with barely a bump as passengers' chitter chatter and excitement increased in volume. With so many families on board, I was amazed that it hadn't been much louder during flight, but was grateful for the calm. While we disembarked, I was still reciting key things from the notes in my head, completely oblivious to the fact that Gary was frozen in his seat.

"You can get up now, Gary. The plane has landed and we have to get off."

"Oh, I know, I just...I thought I saw someone I knew, he looks so much like a cousin of mine but — no, it can't be. He looked familiar, but it couldn't have been anyone I know." The color began to reappear on his face as he stood to retrieve his carry-on and offered to take mine.

"Actually, I was thinking I would take yours. You don't look so hot and it's easier for me to carry the bag than attempt to carry you."

He surprisingly offered little in the way of objection and we were on our way.

It was my turn to do a double take when we stopped to pick up our rental car, which would be at my expense but would make sightseeing a lot more convenient. The girl who took my credit card looked like an old friend, but I chalked up both Gary's confusion and my own to travel fatigue and didn't mention anything.

When we checked into the hotel, I was surprised to find we already had two messages awaiting our arrival. This distraction was enough to keep me from asking for a room with two beds. I'd come to regret that very soon.

Chapter 21

The front desk clerk handed me two keys and two pieces of paper with the messages on them while giving us directions to room 518. Reading the messages in the elevator, I was thrilled to see that my festivities were starting that same night; I was invited to an official Meet and Greet — a three-hour yacht ride on Lake Apopka! I apologized to Gary for standing him up so soon, but he said he understood and that I shouldn't worry about him.

The second message I began to read wasn't nearly as exciting for me. When I saw that it was actually for Gary I handed it to him instead of finishing reading it. I assumed it was from Amanda and he didn't tell me otherwise, but his sly grin was telling.

We got off the elevator just as a family of four was getting on and I suddenly asked Gary, "Are you planning on having kids?"

He was as surprised by the question as I was that I asked it, but he answered quickly, "Someday, maybe, but not for a while." I took in a quick breath because I knew that Amanda was ready and waiting, but I also knew Gary wouldn't have realized how much I knew about their relationship.

When we entered our room we both gasped and our faces reddened.

"There must be some mistake. But I'll take the couch if we can't sort it out."

"Oh no...I forgot all about this."

"You knew?"

"I was supposed to ask for two beds when we got here. Because I took so long to decide if I was bringing a guest they gave me what was left. I can fix it tomorrow if there's another room available, but you should take the bed because this is entirely my fault."

"Not a chance. You need to have a good sleep much more than I do."

"Then we'll both sleep in the bed. I trust you and it should just be for one night. I have to get ready and go. Don't wait up."

I realized that Gary had seen me when I looked at him on the plane, so instead of joining them in the elevator I took the stairs. I was only a couple of rooms down from theirs and was thankful that both Gary and Nat's heads were down reading a pink note when I walked by. I quickly went into my room, where I realized Nat had been carrying another pink slip of paper. It must be a message from the front desk, *I thought.* How am I supposed to figure out what is on her note or if it even matters to me? *It was going to be hard to keep tabs on her here, not knowing the roads, but I had to keep as close to her as possible.*

I called home, explained my predicament, and felt threatened enough to take a risk and play chauffeur for the evening. What you do for love, right?

I rented and picked up a limousine after leaving a message at the front desk to let Nat know she'd have a chauffeur for the evening, compliments of Science in U! I actually pulled up fully dressed as a limo driver as she was walking out of the hotel. I scribbled her name on a piece of paper and got out of the car, thankful that her friend — my second cousin — wasn't with her and that Nat had never seen me close up before.

Arm Farm

Disguising my voice for no more reason than to be able to speak with her again without pause, I called, "Natalie Hartman?"

"Uhh...excuse me, yes, I'm Natalie. I have to tell you, I really don't need a driver. I rented a car and know where the dock is."

"Official orders, Natalie. It'll be my honor to drive you."

Opening the door for her, I was thankful she had let out a small clue as to our destination. Closing the door once she was safely in, I quickly called a number on speed dial – Science in U.

"Yes, I'm driving Natalie Hartman to the dock and I'm new in town. Actually, I'm covering for someone or else she'd have a driver more familiar with the roads, so I am wondering if you would help with directions...great! Yes, I know where that is. So it's just off that street? OK, now I remember. I appreciate your help. Natalie will be there soon."

I got in the limo and drove off, taking my time as I tried to determine how I would get myself on the yacht. As I drove up to the dock, ideas swam through my head but they all seemed too cliché, too much of a spectacle. The winning plan dawned on me as I parked and Nat bounded out of the car to begin chatting with the person taking names. It would be tricky, yes, but that was my specialty.

"My name is Natalie Hartman, I'm here for the..."

"Oh, dear, everyone is. Aren't you excited? I'm thrilled. Is this your first time? I'm part of the conference too and volunteered to take attendance so I can meet everyone before all the events start. That way I'll know who to chose to be my partner for the egg toss."

"Egg toss?"

"Oh, there are tons of get-to-know-you games planned. It'll be great. A little bit different than hitting the books, which will be taking up our time the next few days!"

"And the rest of our lives!" We chuckled.

"I like you, Natalie. Let's be partners. Oh, and I'm Krista Munz. It's nice to meet such a young, promising woman who is still able to relax and make me laugh."

"You're Krista Munz? I've read all of your papers! You look so much younger than the pictures on your books, and so much younger than thirty. I love what you did with your hair! Absolutely, we'll be partners. I'd be honored! But I'll warn you, I haven't tossed an egg in years!"

"You're making me blush. I wanted to do something short and spunky for the conference, something completely unlike me, so I don't know what to think of you liking it. I was just bored of pulling it back into a ponytail every time I get called to a crime scene . This is so much easier. Oh and the games, it's all about the fun of it. If we win we'll rub it in Stephen's face, and if we lose we'll stay out of the way of his ego."

"Who's Stephen?"

"The champion of the game, he's a regular at the conference as you can imagine. He was my partner the first year I attended. I almost made us lose when I sneezed and nearly tripped him! I won't be doing that again! He looks so small and carefree, but he's a competitor."

"Stephen who?" I rephrased. I was in disbelief at the conclusion I was coming to."

"Why, Stephen Pratt, of course. Isn't there only one Stephen in forensics?" She laughed.

Others began arriving so I stepped out of their way, promising Krista that I'd find her when the festivities began.

Leaving behind my drivers' wear, I fit in with the more relaxed attire of the evening. I picked my mark and went for it. "Excuse me, Sam Campbell? Well I'll be..."
"Sorry, I'm not Sam, I..."

"Oh, I'm so sorry. I could've sworn. Sam was a friend of mine in college who was taking the sciences and I thought, remarkable really. You could be twins." He was walking away, closer and closer to the entrance of the yacht and trying to get further from me, but I eagerly followed. "Now I'm not sure which sciences he stuck with, or even if he did. Wow, everything about you screams Sam. Do you mind if I ask your name?"

He turned around just before walking on the ship and told me his name was Stephen Pratt. Perfect! "THE Stephen Pratt? Are you serious! This is so cool. Sam talked about you constantly and you look just like him. I never realized that till now, and I don't think he did either."

"Very good. And you are?"

"I'm Dana Summers, but just call me Dana."

"Well, Dana, I have a party to attend to and I don't think —"

"Oh, of course. But would you mind giving me your autograph first?"

I heard the captain announce for all participants to board immediately. I saw Stephen's hesitation at inviting me to follow him onboard to a table so he could sign on a flat surface. Once completed, I knew all I had to do was excuse myself to the men's room and stay there until the festivities started. It wasn't difficult. I heard Nat chatting as she walked by, just as the yacht's door was closing. I also heard the captain announce departure only moments later. I washed my hands, left the men's room, and followed the crowd.

Chapter 22

The yacht had a smörgåsbord of fruits and vegetables, crackers and cookies, cheese and wine! Nothing was too expensive for the Science in U conference, and it showed. The boat was filled with about a hundred people, all chatting and joyful. I spied a familiar face and was surprised to realize it was my driver. He was chatting it up with a very annoyed-looking Stephen Pratt.

Finally I saw Mr. Pratt escape my driver's clutches and call for attention. When everyone was silent, he announced that the games would begin and that we had ten minutes to pair up; I found Krista in three.

We began with the egg toss. Krista and I won by a single toss; Stephen and his partner Michael Scott came in second. Just as Krista warned, Stephen was playfully furious. Up next was a three-legged race around the deck. Krista and I subtly let Stephen win that one. I saw Dr. Henry Lee for the first time when he was awarded the booby prize for last place. That came as no surprise to anyone, because he was the oldest one on the ship.

When Stephen announced that there would be a game of chess in the cabin in twenty minutes, I took the time to introduce myself to Dr. Lee. "You're my idol — but please don't let Stephen or Krista know. When I learned that you were reviewing cold cases in your free time I wrote you about my parents, Rebecca and Peter Hartman?"

"I have to apologize, I've looked at so many cold cases."

"Oh, I know and I'm grateful you took the time you did to write me back. I was just sorry you didn't find anything."

"Excuse me, the games are beginning and I'm confident I'll do well in this one. I will see you at my lecture tomorrow, no?"

"Yes, of course." As he hurried off I turned to find Krista, who was talking to Stephen. Disheartened by Dr. Lee's rudeness I quickly began to reconsider looking up to him. Stephen and Krista had started taking Dr. Lee's place as my idol. When I found them, they both looked worried.

All the chessboards were set up and we were to play against our partner, but there was a problem: Stephen's partner couldn't be found. Before anyone began to panic we regrouped on the deck, assuming he just hadn't made it back inside after the race.

Everyone on the yacht split into two groups and went in opposite directions, ultimately meeting at the same location. Michael Scott was lying on the deck across from where the race had ended. Then we panicked.

Krista ran to get the ship's nurse while Stephen checked Michael's pulse. He declared it was there but faint; when the nurse came, there wasn't a pulse at all. Stephen immediately took action and told us all to go and stay inside while he, Krista, and — to my surprise — I would gather evidence. The nurse, meanwhile, strapped Michael to a stretcher and told the captain through her walkie-talkie to go back to land ASAP because we had a man in urgent need of medical attention. She disappeared with the body.

"Wow, this really can't be happening. Who is he? Michael Scott...I never heard the name before. And why did you choose me to help?"

Stephen answered, "He's an up-and-comer in the field, but has kept a low profile so far. Krista feels she can trust you and your skillful reputation proceeds you. I'll leave you with Krista to observe while I tackle the other side of the ship. Krista, you have your gear?"

"I never leave home without it." She retrieved her kit and Stephen's from just the other side of the wall, which was the first major clue I missed that something was awry. I was too concerned with securing the crime scene around the drop of blood that I had spotted. I told Krista about the blood as Stephen walked away with his kit.

Krista swabbed the red spatter she saw on her part of the deck and used the Kastle-Meyer test to prove it was blood, and then took a total of six shoe prints. We were efficient and silent as we scoured the remaining side of the deck, and met up with Stephen fairly quickly. He declared he had only found three suspicious items that he felt were worth collecting.

Although we all agreed that someone still on the yacht had done something to Michael, and were nervous at the idea of sharing this with the others, we knew the mystery would be solved a lot more quickly if we did involve everyone. Returning to the crowd, we let Stephen take the lead and he broke the party guests into thirds, each group being led by Stephen, Krista, and myself. I still couldn't believe they trusted me and put me at their level when they had worked in the field for over fifteen years combined. However, I was honored and promised myself to do everything by the book to find our killer.

We decided that whoever had found each piece of evidence would be the best person to describe the circumstance in which it was found. Krista gave me a pep talk and simple instructions before leaving me on my own.

"Let the people in the group talk. Start with as little as possible and listen when they respond and react." Handing me a digital recorder, she continued, "This will record everything for later review, but you need to be careful. If anyone seems suspicious, excuse yourself and Stephen or I will take your place.

We'll be switching groups after a little while if we don't get this figured out soon. You're OK?"

"We'll see. Thanks for trusting me with this. I won't disappoint."

"I know, Natalie, I know," she winked.

I was off to my part of the ship, where a group was waiting. I began with an introduction and then opened the floor to questions. "Excuse me. My name is Natalie and I am here to get any information you may have on this murder. Yes, you in the purple shirt?" As the woman spoke, I scanned the room for anything that looked out of place.

"Is Michael really dead? Wasn't Stephen the last one with him?"

"Yes, and Stephen was, as far as we know."

"Then why is Stephen heading the investigation?" I expected this question, but not the outpouring of frustration that followed. I was so star-struck that I assumed everyone would know Stephen was as innocent as I thought. Stupid of me to make that assumption, but I did.

"No one believes Stephen would be responsible for this, and even if we doubted him he certainly wouldn't have left evidence behind." I fed them the line that I had been instructed and it led in to the discussions that Krista had predicted. I just didn't expect to see the person beside the man asking the next question.

"So you found a lot of evidence?" The voice brought my eye to a short stranger with dark hair and glasses, nothing unusual or distinguishing. What struck me was the man who stood behind him: my driver. As if trying to stay hidden, the driver — dressed differently than I had last seen — avoided eye contact with me and almost crouched behind the questioner. Trying to look deeper into anything I saw as suspicious, I realized I couldn't maintain eye contact. The driver left the crowd and made obvious attempts at staying hidden; I made a mental note to bring him to Krista's attention as I watched his cautious retreat.

The mental note turned out to be unnecessary because my suspicions were my main concern. Krista soon arrived to take my place and took me aside for a consultation. I began telling her of my concern when Stephen joined us and overheard most of my story. They both were surprised that I had been driven to the yacht in a limo, and they explained that no one had hired drivers for guests of the event. I decided I must have been mistaken about who had hired him and pretended to believe it was Professor Matthews who extended the courtesy, but I couldn't convince myself of that. Stephen explained that he'd had a brief encounter with the driver and remembered the name Dana Summers. He was very alarmed that Dana was still on board. We decided to hold him for further questioning, but went back to the matter of the murder.

Chapter 23

Stephen took my story about spotting my driver very seriously and told Krista that he'd take over my place instead of her. They shared a concerned look, and then Krista led me to her group for further questioning.

After we questioned all three groups, we met to discuss our thoughts and agreed to bring in my "driver" as well as Todd, the man he had been trying to hide behind. We also asked one lady to join us for further discussion, and had the entire group gathered together to watch.

"Shouldn't we do this privately?"

"And risk someone jumping ship? No, Natalie, it's because we're not sure it's one of these people who committed the crime. Stephen will be watching the crowd's reactions during our questioning. That way we'll know if we have other people to look at more closely."

"Sounds good. Do I play good cop or bad cop? Or join the crowd?" I was hoping for good cop and that is what Krista assigned me. Although my study of forensics wouldn't qualify me to question a suspect, I loved the opportunity to experience doing so. I was taken aback when Krista handed me a list of questions to ask, as if she had already prepared them. Chalking it up to her being a professional, I let it go.

We started with the woman, whose name was Patty Watts; she'd had an admitted flirtation with the deceased. She was attending the conference as a refresher to get back to working with the FBI. She had taken one year off from the forensic sciences to explore her detective skills, but finally chose to go back to blood splatter analysis. During her gentle interrogation I was too distracted by my driver squirming in his seat to realize Ms. Watts couldn't have committed the crime. Krista, however, quickly caught on and released her from our interrogation. Turning to me before going on to the next suspect, she whispered, "Are you OK?"

"Yeah, sorry. I'm just really nervous. I'll pay more attention while you're questioning Todd, and then I'll tackle Dana."

"Are you sure? I'm very curious, as I'm sure Stephen is, to find out why Dana's on the ship. We need to be very thorough with him."

"I'll start and if you feel I'm off track, I'll gladly let you take over. Trust me, Krista."

"OK, I will." I paid very close attention while Krista did her work and mentally ran through my questions as if I had been a detective for years. Todd cleared his name and we let him go without coming to the conclusion that Dana was our guy, while I became ever more curious as to his presence.

I was next, and not in a good position. I had to get my story straight and be confident in it. By now Nat would have realized that I wasn't hired by the conference, and Stephen would be suspicious as to why I fed him the story about thinking he was an old friend. If I spun the story right, I could only hope that they'd believe me and avoid charging me with kidnapping, although I wasn't sure that charge would stick; Nat had been more than willing to go with me. I certainly wasn't guilty of anything more than that but I was sure to be scrutinized as one of their suspects for murder. Here goes...

Krista confirmed that it was OK to continue questioning, so I started: "Dana Summers, you told me that Science in U hired you. They don't hire drivers. Can you explain that?"

He responded quickly. "My mistake, I assumed that your professor made the arrangements on the conference's behalf. When he gave me the instructions on where to pick you up, I assumed it was all paid for by the conference, not a teacher."

"My professor?" His response took me back a step.

"Yeah...umm...Brian Matthews?"

Krista saw me pause and filled in, "So if you were just hired to drive her here, why did you board the ship?"

"I thought I saw an old college buddy so I got out to say hi but quickly discovered it wasn't the guy I knew. When I asked for his autograph — Stephen's, that is — he took me aboard to find a flat surface to write it on. Before I was able to get off, the boat left the dock. I didn't have any choice except to try to fit in."

"Did you kill Michael?" I took more of a direct route compared to how Krista went about questioning suspects; her reaction told me she was nervous with my question, but it worked.

"Of course I didn't kill him! I don't even know the guy. At the time you're saying he would have been attacked," — this was the first indication of his innocence, as Michael wasn't technically "attacked." — "I was getting detached from my partner after the three-legged race."

"And who was your partner?"

"Actually, it was Todd."

Before I could continue questioning Dana, Krista let him go even though I wanted to know more about him. It was only fair, though, as we believed he had proved his innocence. Krista motioned for me to follow her and Stephen after I heard Stephen advise everyone to stay put.

When we arrived in the deserted captain's room, Stephen closed the door behind me and then asked what we all thought. I had to confess that I was still concerned with Dana, but that was something I had to get over.

"It just sounds like such a pleasant misunderstanding that I wouldn't be worried about it. But if you're that worried, Krista or I will make sure you get back to the hotel safely. Did you notice anything unusual, Krista?"

Her smile in such a serious situation puzzled me, but she admitted she noticed nothing.

"So what do we do now?" I sounded less-than-confident and a ton naive, but they were respectful and pretended to expect that I would ask that.

"Well, I'm glad you asked, Natalie. Let's go back to the crowd and see if we can figure this out." We returned to a muted but chatty crowd that was anxious to know what we were going to do next. Stephen asked if anyone had anything to confess or to point out to us. It was then that it dawned on me: I knew who the murderer was, and so did a handful of onlookers, by the sight of them. I tapped Krista on the shoulder and she took me aside, grinning. "Yes?"

"I know who did it. It had to be the captain."

"Are you sure?"

"A hundred percent. He was the only one with the opportunity to do it. And two of the people interviewed confirmed it. Isn't that weird?"

"What would be his motive?"

Recalling the events of the night, the captain's motive came to me. "Patty gave us motive. The captain is Michael's brother, and wanted full control of the cruise business. He was mad that Michael was taking half of the profits but always off doing his own thing, putting forth very little effort to keep the business on its feet."

"OK, let's hear what the others are saying."

"Shouldn't we tell Stephen and have the captain arrested?"

"Let's listen, Natalie. We'll see what the others are saying and then go from there." I was confident in my findings and couldn't comprehend why Krista was acting so casual. It worried me.

It turned out that the others were supporting my findings, coming to the same conclusion I had, or at least offering more proof to back it up. The proof kept coming until suddenly everyone stopped speaking. Michael appeared behind the crowd, with his brother the captain beside him, and the crowd's surprise stopped everything. Gasps were heard over the chatter as the crowd turned to see Michael alive and well. Stephen caught everyone's attention again by congratulating the group on a well-played murder mystery.

Looking from Stephen to Krista, I realized that they had been in on it the whole time. I was mystified by the elaborate scheme and started the applause of appreciation. I joined the crowd and chatted with everyone until the boat returned to land. Then I remembered my biggest concern: getting back to the hotel. Dana caught up with me, apologizing for his mistake again and again, and offered to make it up to me by driving me home. Krista came to my rescue and Dana drove his limousine away empty. Krista and I chatted a bit and then she offered to drive me to the hotel.

Chapter 24

When I returned to the hotel room, the drive courtesy of Science in U with Krista behind the wheel this time, Gary was sound asleep. Although I had to get up early for workshops, I was revved from the adrenaline boost of the murder mystery. I dressed for bed in the dark and carefully climbed into bed with a book. When I turned on my light I saw Gary sleeping peacefully and wondered what the message was from Amanda. Without cracking open my book, I left the bed and snuck over to the garbage can. I saw right away that there were only two pink slips in it but had to take them both to bed to read them in the light.

Gary's note surprised me. It wasn't from Amanda at all — it was from Professor Matthews. I couldn't believe that he was asking Gary to look after me. He was so sweet and the knowledge of this made me blush once again, but also frightened me that Amanda hadn't left any messages yet. I wanted to call Amanda to ask for updates on my case but decided it was too late at night. Instead I escaped to the bathroom with my cell phone, closed the door, and left a message for Detective Brock. My message was brief and I didn't leave the hotel number for fear of Gary answering the phone when Detective Brock called back. Alternatively, I said I would try him at a later time.

I knew I had to relax and get some sleep so I went back to bed, read a chapter, and fell fast asleep before even turning the light off. Gary's hand venturing its way up my shirt and under my bra startled me awake. I gasped and looked towards him, realized he was still asleep, and removed his hand from my body. He did the same thing again — this time more forcefully — before I drifted off, so I got up and went to the couch. I'd have to ask for a new room in the morning.

When my alarm sounded, I quickly turned it off so that it didn't wake Gary, but saw that he was already up and showered.

"I hope I didn't wake you, Nat. How come you moved to the couch?"

He wasn't even aware of what he had done just hours earlier. Deciding to be casual about it and not wanting to risk all the relationships involved, I told him I realized my alarm would wake him in the bedroom. "I didn't think you'd want to be up this early. Since you are, did you want to join me for breakfast?"

"Natalie, I'm in Florida. I'm not going to spend my visit sleeping in a hotel room! And I would love to have breakfast with you. We could save time by ordering in room service," Gary suggested.

The thought of eating alone with Gary made me anxious. "Actually, I thought we could go out. I got up early enough to allow for breakfast, as long as you don't mind dropping me off when we're done."

"Of course! I wanted to get a good start on my exploring anyway. I thought you could catch me up on the excitement of last night. You were telling some funny stories in your sleep —"

I blushed, not realizing I had been so restless and talkative in the early hours of my sleeping.. "Oh my, I'm so sorry. I never realized I talked in my sleep. I guess with all the excitement I wasn't sleeping as soundly as I thought. I hope I didn't keep you up."

"It was actually quite amusing so I didn't mind."

"I'll just grab a quick shower and we'll go."

I was fast in the shower and even faster at breakfast. Gary seldom interrupted, so I was able to fill him in on most of the details from the night before. He was in complete awe at my making such quick friends with Stephen and Krista and told me how lucky I was.

"So tell me," I began on the way to the conference, "any big plans for you today?"

"Mostly just sightseeing today. Thought I'd pick up a few souvenirs. We are still on for Disney World before we go home, right?"

"Wouldn't miss it. Maybe I'll see if Stephen and Krista can join us. Here we are, gotta run, thanks Gary."

I was out of the car and up the stairs so quickly that I didn't recognize the man who held the door open for me as my limo driver.

After the close call on the boat I decided that trying to convince Stephen to invite me to the workshops would not be a good idea. I'd have to find something to do with my days while Nat was learning new methods to find me. I wanted to follow Gary but decided it was too risky, and chose to return to my hotel room instead. I was tempted to return home but decided against that, too. It would be easier to have Nat disappear in Florida than back at home. But it was simple to miss a flight and that's what might have to happen to her if she was on to me. Even though I had been told not to cause harm, I wanted to so badly. Then it would all be over and my life could continue.

In my hotel room I was bored to exhaustion, so I decided to tour the city in search of the perfect place to dispose of a body — you know, just in case — but first made a quick stop a couple rooms down from mine. I knew I had to keep a low profile, but I also knew no one would be home.

Chapter 25

Stephen got right into discussing bone marrow and saliva, the forensic science equivalent of meat and potatoes, at the beginning of the day, knowing that each workshop attendee was fully qualified to follow along. During our breaks I mixed in with others instead of bothering Stephen and Krista as almost everyone else was doing. The information was extensive, but revitalizing at the same time.

Dr. Lee's presentation was amazing, but I still didn't like his attitude towards everyone.

At the end of the day, we were given the task of preparing a presentation to tell the class why we were there, why we were studying forensic sciences, and what we hoped to learn in the next day and a half, giving us half a day's lead time to prepare our reasons for being there. I had already learned a lot from the cruise, so I knew it wouldn't take long for me to prepare my presentation.

When the workshops let out, Krista offered to drive me back to the hotel and I accepted. On the way, I told her that Gary wanted to meet her and Stephen, to which she said she'd be happy to meet a friend of mine. We went up to the hotel room only to find it empty but ransacked. I began trembling, knowing that Gary would have been out all day and that housekeeping would have already cleaned up long before.

"Are you OK?"

"Someone was in here. Krista, I'm being followed."

"Now, let's calm down and talk about this. We can't jump to any drastic conclusions."

"You don't understand…" After double-checking that we were alone, I began to tell her the story. Before getting too far in, Krista hushed me and escorted me out of the room.

"If you're serious this guy could have bugged your room. Let's go out for a drink and you can tell me all you know. I'll call Stephen and see if he's free to listen, too."

"No, I don't want to bother him. I feel bad even burdening you with something that may be nothing."

She replied with something I didn't want to acknowledge: "If this guy followed you all the way here it's something we need to take seriously. You'll be OK, especially with Stephen and me on your side, but you can tell me before we decide whether to take it to Steve."

Krista brought me to an out-of-the-way bar that she promised made the best dessert in town and was never crowded. We sat at a corner table and ordered some cocktails while we studied the menus. Krista already knew she wanted the Deep Chocolate Escape and recommended I either try that or the Caramel Apple Supreme. I decided on the latter after she promised that she'd let me try a bite of hers.

While we waited for our desserts, we sipped our drinks and I dished the details. The only interruption was the bartender with our desserts and a second drink for us both. When I finished my story, Krista remained silent. After a while, I commented on the tremendously delicious desserts and asked her if she'd mind coming back to the bar with Gary and Stephen another time. She said she wouldn't mind at all.

"I'm worried for you and want to help but don't even know where to start. If these events started happening in Boston, that's where most of the clues will be. I say we should go back to the hotel and check for prints, then I'll have them sent back to

Detective Brock and have him compare them with the samples he took."

"What if it's Gary? What if he gets back to the room before we do?" I hadn't even told her about my parents' deaths, didn't think they connected with the other happenings — or at least not at that moment.

"Let's go and worry about what we know and what we have confirmed. I'll call Stephen and let him know you won't have your presentation done —"

"No, I still will. It won't take me long and I think I will need to concentrate on something other than this situation in order to sleep tonight. I won't let this affect my studies."

"Natalie, don't put your work ahead of your safety. Never do that. But follow your heart and do what's best for you."

"Thanks, Krista. I appreciate your listening and support. I bet you weren't expecting this much when you befriended me."

"I never know what to expect when I come to this conference. Let's go," she said, half-smiling.

Stephen met us at the hotel after Krista phoned him to take a rain check on dinner. Gary arrived after Stephen and was oblivious to the mess our room was in, as he was caught up with being in the same room as Stephen and Krista. I made the introductions and continued cleaning up the fingerprint dust with Krista while Stephen explained why they were there.

"Sorry for taking over your room, but we knew a hotel room would be a great place for sample prints and Natalie volunteered hers. She knew you'd be excited to meet us so we figured you could look past the mess." Gary took Stephen's story as truth, for which we were very thankful. I couldn't bear lying to Gary but it would be worse if he knew the truth, so Stephen had offered to give him our cover story. Krista, as if to confirm Stephen's tale, excused herself to retrieve her fingerprinting kit.

"Do you mind if I take your fingerprints, Gary, to be able to eliminate them from our collection?"

"I'd be honored," he said after just a small hesitation. I caught it, but the moment was so brief that Krista and Stephen didn't notice. I went to the bathroom to clean the sink faucets as well as the toilet lever and seat; we were crossing our fingers that the culprit had used the bathroom during his rampage. It didn't take long for Krista to join me and whisper, "Are you OK? Did you want your own room or to stay at my place?"

I whispered back, "No, I have to be strong and I don't want Gary to get any more suspicious than he must already be. I'll be OK here. Thanks, though. You've been really great."

"All right, we're outta here then. See you in the morning, Natalie." I followed Krista out to say goodbye to Stephen. Our goodbye interrupted a deep debate between Gary and Stephen about a paper Stephen had written. I, too, had read the paper and had an opinion, but knew Stephen was exhausted by the look in his eyes, so I kept quiet. Stephen abruptly ended his conversation with Gary, said his goodbyes, and exited, leaving Gary on an intellectual high and me in a nervous state.

"Well, I have a presentation to prepare and then have to go to bed. What do you have planned?"

"I can help you with your presentation. I owe you — they are awesome! I can't believe I met Stephen! Wow, you're so lucky."

"Thanks. No, I'm good for the presentation. I know what to write. I just have to sit down and work on it. Why don't you call Amanda and tell her who you just met?"

"Yeah, that's what I'll do. You're sure you're all right?"

For a second I thought he meant because of what happened — what *was* happening — and not the presentation. "Yeah, I'll be fine. Just ask Amanda how my kitty is doing. I know it's only been one day, but he's my baby." I sat at the desk in the room and set up my laptop; I was so consumed in my thoughts that I never even heard Gary leave. When I took a breath and noticed that I was alone, I got worried.

I tried to convince myself that Gary had stepped out to call Amanda and give me some quiet time to write. In a way I was thankful but also irritated; however, I knew I was the one choosing to keep him in the dark about my case, so I'd have to deal with it. He returned just as I was closing my laptop, feeling fulfilled at the thought of opening up to the class in Florida. I hid so much from everyone in Boston that it was going to be liberating to be honest with other budding scientists. I never realized how relevant my presentation was to my current situation.

Gary came back and filled me in on how my cat was and how Amanda was managing without him. He finally seemed a little sad, missing Amanda, but it would only be four more days so I didn't mention it. We went to bed and both slept peacefully, with Gary mentioning in the morning that he hadn't heard me mutter a word during the night.

Damn it, they are both helping her now. Stupid, stupid, stupid. And careless! Although they wouldn't find my prints anywhere, I knew I was risking too much and had to lie low. I thought lying low would be easier to do back in Boston, but my "boss" wouldn't allow my early return. Eyes needed to be on Nat and that's what I had promised to provide. I didn't understand why I always fell in love with such demanding people but knew I had to do what was asked, or I'd be alone again. I did, despite the risk of a fight with my "boss," change my flight so that I wouldn't be returning on the same plane as Nat.

In my old age I was letting my personal interests tempt me instead of being extra careful. I'd never been like that before and had to try to go back to my old ways. I had a lot to consider, a lot to plan, and a lot of time to do so while hiding in my hotel room. It was time to catch up on my daytime talk shows while I figured out my next move.

Chapter 26

I confirmed with Stephen and Krista the next morning that I had been able to get my presentation done with no problem at all. Stephen warned me that he would call on me to present right after our first break. The speeches before the first break bored me, as each person talked about how television shows like *Dexter*, the *CSI*'s, and *Bones* all led them to the sciences. Although I enjoyed these shows, I often laughed at how ridiculously they solved their crimes, and knew that thousands of students changed their majors only to find out that the sciences weren't as Hollywood as their favorite shows.

I could tell that Krista and Stephen expected the content of most of the presentations right up until I presented my work.

"I'm here today for more complex reasons than any of you touched on thus far. I've been interested in the sciences and solving crimes ever since I found my mother murdered in my home when I was seven. My father's body was discovered in another room later that day by police." The crowd reacted as I assumed they would, but when Krista began to stand I motioned for her to sit back down. I needed to get through my speech without pause. I continued to summarize how broken I had felt after finding my mother and hearing about my father. The speech continued past the time limit I had been given, but no one dared to stop me and I concluded without shedding a single tear.

Only minutes after I finished, the bell rang for lunch and when it did the whole class seemed to approach me. I was grateful when Stephen asked for everyone to leave and for me to stay behind before anyone had a chance to offer me condolences or ask a question. I wanted to hear what Krista and Stephen thought of my confession before I tackled anyone else.

"That was compelling and extremely brave of you, Natalie. Your presentation was much more interesting, but also more heartbreaking than everyone else's. Are you OK to join the group for lunch or did you want to go out separately?" Stephen spoke first.

"I'll be fine with the group, I need to face them and be OK with it."

"But you don't, Nat. This afternoon we only have two more presentations to hear and then we review the fingerprint findings in groups of three. If it's easier for you, Krista, you and me can form a group if you want."

"I don't want to be singled out for this. I just needed to fulfill the assignment truthfully and this venue gave me the chance to do that. I want to eat lunch with everyone and answer all of their questions now, if that's OK."

"That's perfectly OK. Now let's go so we don't get the crappy sandwiches, or nothing at all."

Stephen and Krista were becoming great friends of mine and weren't nearly as "by the book" as their published papers made them seem. They saw the personal side of everything and understood that first, then processed the evidence knowing they were dealing with someone's friend, son or daughter, sister or brother. They investigated people, not just victims. As each session passed, I found myself wanting to be more like them, and knew that I could be.

I separated from Krista and Stephen once we hit the buffet and was actually invited to cut in front of the person I related to best in the class. Trevor was one of the two remaining students who hadn't given his presentation yet and he confessed he was a bit nervous to follow mine. "The truth is, Natalie, my story is just like all the others. I fell in love with *Dexter* during the first episode and began studying blood splatter from then on. Nothing dramatic happened to me. It's just something I thought I would be good at."

"I don't wish anything that dramatic on anyone, Trevor. Each of us has our strengths and it doesn't matter *how* we go about finding them, only that we do. If blood's your thing and you're good at it, then it's a good thing you watched *Dexter* and discovered your interest so quickly."

"My parents thought I was nuts. They wanted me to play sports but I couldn't see myself getting paid so highly for entertaining. They taught me values and I couldn't ignore their teachings...sorry, I don't mean to be talking about my parents so much. I'm so sorry about yours."

"It's OK, really. It happened years ago and although it still affects me, it doesn't hurt to hear others talk about their parents. It makes me realize how great mine were, how great they would have been today, and how proud they would be of me." We reached the table and I grabbed a turkey sub, then a can of Pepsi. "Where would you like to sit?" I asked Trevor.

"Anywhere is fine with me. I'm right behind you," he replied, carrying a tuna wrap and a Coke. "I wouldn't take you for a Pepsi girl, Natalie," he commented with a smile.

I shot a teasing look of distaste at his selection. "I couldn't choke that other stuff down if someone wanted to pay me. Pepsi girl, born and raised."

We found two empty seats and he rushed to pull my chair out, waiting for me to sit before he did. I could barely get the sub to my mouth before another workshop attendee at the table interrupted with a question. "Is your story true or did you make all that up to be different?"

Trevor actually fielded that question. "How rude can you be? Do you think someone is going to pour his or her heart out like that and be lying? Get out of here, Sam."

"All right, all right. I just thought...I wanted to be sure. If there's anything I can do to make it up to you…"

I spoke this time, "Just let us eat and don't be so abrupt next time." I turned and took a bite, barely swallowing before someone else approached.

"I'm so sorry to have heard that, Natalie. It's scary to think something so terrible happened to someone so sweet and smart. I hope you solve their murders some day."

"Me, too. Thanks, Chad."

When we turned to see a line-up of eager classmates wanting to extend their condolences, Trevor interrupted, "Let's get out of here, get some privacy." We went out to the hallway and found a bench near a window. When I sat down and began unwrapping my sub again I noticed his eyes on me and asked what he was looking at.

Chapter 27

"Do I have mayo on my cheek or something?" I
submitted with light humor.

"Nothing like that at all. I just..." And then Trevor
reached out and touched my cheek ever so slightly. Embarrassed,
I turned to look out the window and heard him whisper that I was
beautiful. While I was sorting out what to say, Trevor leaned in
and kissed me, making me realize it was the one time I was
thankful I was speechless.

It didn't take long for me to start kissing back. It seemed
like only seconds passed before the crowd of our classmates was
emerging from the doors and coming towards us. Although the
physical kiss lasted only seconds the escape, the relief, and the
confusion of it would last much longer. We quickly went back to
eating our lunch. I was almost thankful for the interruption and to
be getting back to class.

Although I asked very few questions of my classmates, I
had to answer a lot before class started again. Most were civil
about it; some were very kind and others were less than tactful.
To them I put up a strong front, pretending that my situation was
an important case even though the cops had practically stopped
investigating it years before. I had to be objective, couldn't let
myself be sensitive to sharing my story anymore, and I was not
only determined to solve the case but to spread the word of
closed, unsolved cases. I owed it to my parents and I owed it to
myself.

Arm Farm

I opened my can of Pepsi, not realizing it would soon make me the center of attention one more time. Trevor took center stage first and admitted that he had something prepared but had been inspired by my bravery to tell us something other than what he had planned. I was thankful he did, as he opened up and confessed to being a victim of sexual assault as a kid. I was shocked; the class was silent but everyone was grateful that Trevor hadn't given the speech we'd heard so many times before.

The confessions only snowballed and the class quickly became loud with excitement right into the last speech. Patty — the woman I had interviewed on the cruise — was embarrassed to begin her story by letting us know that she got into the field simply because her parents were both scientists. She followed their path but with her own personal twist. It impressed me that she was completing all of the assignments without complaint and she was doing them well.

When we split up into teams of three to discuss the fingerprints, I was pleased to be on Patty's team but nervous to have Trevor join us. Patty was knowledgeable but not arrogant and let Trevor and I do a lot of the work, in turn letting us learn from our mistakes. Trevor was very nonchalant and made no mention of our prior activities, but his accidental touches on my hand sent tingles through my body.

After the class completed our fingerprint analyses, we brought them to Krista for input into the database borrowed from the local police department. Stephen asked me for my can of soda but only if it was empty, he specified. I heard the whispers as I was being named the teacher's pet and couldn't believe how immature some of the conference attendees were. To think that they paid the fees to be here and all they were doing was making a mockery of themselves was discouraging. I hoped I would never have to work with some of these people again. When I told Stephen that I was finished with the soda, he took the can from me with a gloved hand.

"Are you a germaphobe, Mr. Pratt?" It was the rude guy from lunch, and his "posse" hadn't gone unnoticed in the fiasco. I thought Stephen would be upset at the question, but he turned it around to his benefit.

"Tell me, would you enter a crime scene and leave your own evidence behind for processing? Not only would that be a complete waste of time and money for the city but it would keep *your* name on the suspect list until you could find a reliable alibi. I would hope most of you learned that in your intro forensics class and that I don't find evidence from a single one of you at my next crime scene." That embarrassed the rude guy and his friends immediately, and they kept quiet for the remainder of the class.

While Krista entered the prints in the database, I watched her with anxious eyes. I expected to see something in her face if she matched the prints from the hotel to someone in the class. She remained calm so I had to remain attentive; if she did show anything, I didn't see it.

Stephen continued to explain how crucial it is to lift prints correctly. He went on to describe how particular the courts were about matching as many points on a fingerprint as possible when trying someone for a crime; most times you needed at least twelve. He showed us an example of lifting a print off the can incorrectly and asked the class if anyone had caught his mistake.

I raised my hand, feeling a bit disappointed that we were learning about something so elementary. Stephen called on a few others who thought they had outsmarted the expert, but he advised them all that they were incorrect. With my hand still raised I began second-guessing my answer, thinking it just as obvious as every other attempt. By the time Stephen asked for my answer I was about to put my hand back down. I answered anyway, and he smiled in response. "I'm glad you thought of that, Natalie, but that's not the answer I'm actually looking for. OK, answer me this class: what other type of evidence can you get from a soda can?"

That one was easy and the class just shouted out the answer: "Saliva!"

"OK, now what did I do wrong with getting this fingerprint?"

The look of dawning came over all of us, but only one voice sounded. "You destroyed the chance of obtaining other evidence when you tilted it."

"That's right. It's not always about how you get the one piece of evidence, but *how you process* all the evidence you can."

Krista took that moment to take Stephen aside and adjourned the class for a ten-minute break. This time they specified that we needed to take our break outside of the classroom. We thought it strange but left without dispute. I think I was the most curious of all and my attitude showed this. Trevor tried conversing with me and I just sat silent, worried about what Krista had found.

Chapter 28

It turned out the dismissal from class had nothing to do with Krista's findings. She and Stephen were simply setting up for the remainder of the afternoon and didn't want spies.

The rest of the afternoon touched on enough challenges that it renewed my faith in the conference. The workshop's earlier simplicity was intended to throw us off our game — and it certainly had.

Krista and Stephen invited me to stay for a minute after class just to confirm our plans for supper. It didn't take long and Trevor met me on the way out.

"Any plans for supper? I thought —"

"Sorry, Trevor, I do have plans. I'm...I promised my friend who came with me that we'd go to the Hard Rock Cafe tonight."

"Boyfriend?"

"No, no," I laughed. "Friend, boyfriend of my best friend."

"So he wouldn't mind that I insisted on joining you."

I wasn't sure I did the best thing, but I couldn't bear to reject him. "We're eating at six at the Hard Rock Cafe on Universal Boulevard. I have to run but meet us there if you'd like." I ran out unsure if I should have advised him that Stephen and Krista were coming. I figured he would find out soon enough.

When I arrived at the hotel Gary was ready and waiting to leave, excited beyond belief to see Stephen and Krista again. He had dressed to the nine's and his usual mess of blond curls were brushed perfectly in place. The fact that he'd never been to a Hard Rock Cafe paled dramatically compared to seeing the celebrated forensic scientists.

"I know you're anxious, Gary. I just have to change and then we'll go," I told him on my way to the bathroom. The can of soda was hitting me so hard I didn't have time to take my change of clothes with me. I told him from the bathroom about Trevor joining us, but didn't think it was necessary to justify it or mention our kiss. I planned to wear my red pumps with my casual little black dress to match Trevor's six-foot height and Gary's formal wear. I would leave my hair down.

After relieving myself, I went into my suitcase for a change of clothes and grimaced at the stench. I was hit with the sharp smell of aftershave that I knew didn't belong to Gary. It hit my lungs and I began coughing as Gary hustled to get me a glass of water while I sat on the bed, leaving the suitcase open. When I was able to verbalize my words instead of coughing them, I asked Gary if that was his aftershave spilled all over my clothes, hoping my suspicion was mistaken and that it was in fact his.

"No, I don't wear aftershave. If I wear anything it's got to be Polo, and that's not Polo. What's going on, Natalie? You look like you've seen a ghost."

I had to confess, to tell him everything. I knew I could trust him now but didn't want to hurt him. He would be crushed to think I had considered him a suspect. He was waiting for an answer but had no idea what to expect.

I told him everything, or at least all that I knew, which wasn't a whole lot. The story was scary to everyone who heard it. Gary sat in silence; the only look on his face was disbelief — not guilt or shame — simply unbelieving. A full minute of silence went by before he even reacted, but the minute felt much longer.

Time was running thin, so I made the decision to move for the door in lieu of changing. Gary followed me.

While alone in the elevator, he quickly told me how sorry he was to hear about everything that had taken place and offered to help with anything I needed. We met the crew in the lobby and I started to make quick introductions, but everyone began conversing like old friends.

When there was an opportunity, I blurted out that Gary knew about my stalker and explained the reason I hadn't changed clothes. Things quieted down a notch with that and everyone immediately offered to stay in.

"No, we can't, I won't let this guy ruin my experience here. Besides, I told Trevor to meet us at the restaurant and we've already kept him waiting. Please don't tell him about the stalker so we don't dwell on it all night."

Everyone agreed to keep quiet about my situation and we hopped into the cab and were off. Gary didn't shut up the whole way and I was surprised to see him like that, but of course there is that old cliché 'there's a first time for everything'. His excited chitchat left me in my own silence to wonder about all the possible explanations for what was happening. I knew that although we wouldn't be talking about my stalker over dinner, each of us would be thinking about him. I could see in Gary's eyes that although he was conversing about "hypotheticals" he was trying to figure out how he could help me. Krista's sympathetic looks came too often and deepened too quickly with intensity.

When we arrived at the restaurant, I took a deep breath — a *very* deep breath — before stepping out of the cab. Steve and Gary sped along toward the restaurant and left Krista with me to make sure I was OK.

"As OK as I can be, I guess."

"I'm so sorry. It's so difficult to be in your shoes. I know, I was there once, not too long ago."

"You were?!"

"Part of the reason I came into this field was because I saw how stalking cases were handled. Mine was sent to cold cases within months. My case wasn't a priority until the police discovered it was linked to a serial stalker and then they found him."

"My God, I'm so sorry, Krista. I don't wish this on anyone."

We caught up to the boys who had overheard my last comment and chuckled, "We can go eat somewhere else," Gary commented with a smile.

"And miss your ever-increasing excitement trip? Not a chance!"

Krista and Stephen tried to hide their reaction but I egged them on by laughing myself. Although the tension remained, my laughter eased it.

While we waited in line to be seated, Trevor approached and told us he already had our table. Fortunately he had chosen a booth that fit everyone. I sat between him and Gary, while Stephen and Krista sat across from us. Trevor occasionally squeezed my thigh when he was sure no one was looking. I was careful not to react.

For the next hour I let loose, had a few much-needed drinks, and enjoyed my company and myself. In a way, I was thankful to have Gary in the know; I felt more secure and comfortable as a result. We did tread carefully, but still enjoyed our evening. I made Trevor a promise that I'd call him when I got back to the hotel. He handed me a note with his room number before he made his exit.

It wasn't until we were in a cab that we spoke again of my trauma, and the realization of it hit me harder than before. Krista confessed that she had noticed a man watching us the entire time we were at dinner. She didn't want me to be alarmed but it was too late; I had seen him too.

"Holy shit, why didn't you mention it in there so I could confront him?"

"And ruin a perfectly good meal?! Natalie, I've been there, I've regrettably accused complete strangers many times and still hate that I did that. We weren't there long. He could have just been weird. Have you seen him before?"

"I don't think so." Something was only vaguely familiar about him, not enough to warrant an attack as Krista warned. "Thanks, Krista. And it has been a stupendous night. I can't thank you guys enough — for dinner, the conference, and for being so great about everything."

Stephen picked up on the idea of distraction, however slight, and asked, "Have you been learning anything useful?"

"Tons! And the stuff I already know is good to review so that I understand its importance. I loved hearing the real stories of how people became interested in the field. Although some are obviously terrifying, they are real. I just feel selfish that I'm starting to want to solve my own case before my parents…"

"Natalie, don't think that at all. We're going to find your stalker in no time. You leave your parents' case to me right now and you concentrate on your studies and staying safe. I'll get online tomorrow and find out anything I can," Gary promised. "I'll also take you where you need to go and pick you up when you're done. You'll be sick of me before we go home."

"Thanks, Gary. I'm so sorry I ever thought you were the stalker. You're absolutely right, Krista, I can't accuse everyone I know. I need to find some evidence and go from there. Anyone up for a nightcap? My treat."

Stephen replied that he needed to get back to prepare for the final day of classes, to which Krista agreed, but when they dropped us off at the hotel, Gary accepted my invitation. He admitted that he wanted a little one-on-one time to figure out where to start on his investigation. Instead of going back out, we agreed to a beer in the hotel bar.

Chapter 29

Before long I was trembling and through with my first beer. I was about to ask the bartender for another, but Gary stopped me, "You need to be alert tomorrow, not hungover."

"I know, it's just the further I go the more real it seems."

"Let's go to bed then. I have some ideas on what to do. Hopefully I'll find a lead from at least one of my ideas and be able to follow it through." He gulped his last bit of beer, left a ten on the table, and we retreated to the room, realizing once again that I had forgotten to ask for a room with a second bed. I figured it wasn't that big of deal and sucked it up.

I couldn't let what he said about working on my parents' case go and didn't want him wasting time on a lead I'd already exhausted so I asked, "What's your idea?"

"I'm going to search newspapers for any mention of your parents' murder."

"There are a lot but they lead nowhere. I don't want to disappoint you but I don't want you spinning your tires, either."

"Let me do it, I'll go at it differently than you did."

"How so?"

"Have you looked at the reporters who covered the story?"

My look told him I hadn't and my mind started to wander but I decided to reel it in and call it a night, confident Gary was on to something. "I'll take the couch tonight so you can sleep in."

"Don't be ridiculous. If you insist on us not sleeping together, you take the bed. I'll surf on my laptop for a bit and crash on the couch."

I wasn't going to argue. "Thanks Gary. Tomorrow I'll make sure I ask for another room." When he turned his back I smiled with relief; I had the bed, I was alone, and most importantly, Trevor was expecting my call.

When our phone call ended, I couldn't sleep because my brain and nerves were tingling with excitement. I decided to go talk to Gary but when I walked through the open doorway from the bedroom to the living room and saw him already passed out I had a much better idea. Still holding the note with Trevor's room number on it, I sneaked out of our room and hurried down the hall.

I knocked quietly on Trevor's door, still unsure exactly what I expected or even if Trevor was alone or already asleep. I was about to turn back when he opened the door. "Natalie."

"Sorry, I couldn't sleep."

"Don't apologize, neither could I —" and that's when I did something I've never done before. I kissed him — hard. With the embrace, I pushed him back into the room and closed the door. "You're not bunking with someone are you?" I asked, out of breath.

He didn't elaborate, just said no and began undressing me, then told me if I wanted to stop he would. I didn't say a word. I wanted the release, the escape, the distraction. I wanted Trevor even if it was just for one night. I wanted it to be just one night, nothing long-term. I thought he understood that.

I lay awake for the rest of the night as worst-case scenarios took over from the adrenaline rush and ran rampant through my head. I had no idea what Gary had planned for the next day and he refused to tell me all of the details. Trevor slept soundly and I was easily annoyed. Each of his snores vibrated down my spine, his exhales shivered back up.

"Gary?!"

"No, Trevor," Trevor said groggily with a sense of disappointment.

"No, I mean...what's he going to think when I'm not in bed? I have to go." I found my clothes, embarrassed that I had worn my flannel pajama pants and an old shirt to a booty call, and dressed. "Dammit. I don't have my key. I don't have time to run down and get a second before Gary wakes up," I whined when I looked at the clock. When I opened Trevor's door and saw the complimentary newspaper, I decided on my plan.

I went to my hotel room, and abashed, knocked on the door to be let in and heard Gary startle inside.

"What, Gary, is something wrong?" I asked when he opened the door.

"You tell me. What are you doing out here?"

"I was awake so thought I'd get the paper, but I locked myself out. You were sleeping so soundly when I crept by, I hope I didn't wake you."

"Thank God, you're OK. No, you were quiet as a mouse. I just pee a lot when I drink beer and was worried when I couldn't find you. I gotta go." He ran to the bathroom and I sat on the bed, turned on the light, then gathered my clothes and waited for the bathroom. Gary came out and went to his laptop.

"You don't have to stay up. I turned off the alarm to let you sleep in."

"Nat, I'm here for you, I'm taking you to class and just figure I'll get a head start on the day."

"Did you have any more questions?"

"Not right now but I may before you go." I came back out after turning on the shower and rested my hand on his shoulder. He looked up and apologized for being so absorbed he didn't notice me, explaining he thought he was on to something but refused to say what. I glanced at the screen and saw something that terrified me: a reflection of the man we'd seen at the Hard

Rock Cafe. I gasped and Gary calmly asked what was wrong. I couldn't speak; I merely turned around to see an empty hotel room. I realized then how truly tired I was and fell to my knees.

Chapter 30

"Natalie, are you OK?"

"I'm sorry, I thought I saw the guy from the restaurant in the monitor. I know why I recognized him. He's been everywhere I've been. In fact, I think — oh my God — Gary!"

"Natalie, what's wrong?"

"I can't be sure…no, I can't jump to that conclusion so quickly. Krista was right, I'm accusing everyone instead of presuming each one innocent."

"You've been under a lot of stress, it's to be expected. Maybe you shouldn't go to your workshop today. Maybe we should just go home."

"If you were in my shoes, would you give up?"

"Of course not. Nothing would keep me away from this conference, especially the last day."

"Then why would you think I'd give up? I'm going, nothing will stop me." I smiled at Gary and escaped to the shower. When I got out, I apologized for being so abrupt with him but realized he understood. While he showered, I finished putting up my hair with time to spare. Although his laptop tempted me, I refrained. I didn't want to snoop or get myself worked up again.

Gary emerged from the bathroom looking hot and seasonal, fully dressed in khaki shorts and a camouflage t-shirt just as the phone rang. "I got it," I told him. It was Amanda, so I told her that Gary knew everything before passing on the phone to him.

I tried not to eavesdrop, but he wouldn't let me leave the room without him. I picked up my Stephen King book and immersed myself in the life of Randy and his diabolical problems with gremlins and goblins.

When Gary got off the phone, he stood silent and I couldn't decide whether to break the silence or continue reading my book. I took the oblivious approach and kept reading. I finished the chapter, looked at my watch, put the book away, and looked at Gary. "Are you ready?"

"We're pregnant."

I wasn't sure how he wanted me to react but I picked up on the fact that he'd said, "We're pregnant" instead of "Amanda's pregnant." I knew he had been planning to wait to start a family, but I sensed they were excited all the same — or, at least Gary was — and I knew that this was what Amanda had been wanting for a long time. I suddenly realized why she had been so emotional lately. I went with my gut and said, "Congratulations!"

Gary beamed and his smile then matched the thrill in his dark eyes. I jumped up and hugged him, promising to call Amanda when we returned, and apologized for trying to rush him out. He was glowing and seemed not to care about anything except his new family — of course I couldn't blame him.

In the car I told him not to worry about me today. "I know you have a lot more on your mind now than to be bothered with my issues."

"Natalie, if we were back in Boston I would have to say you're right — but we're not. There's nothing I can do for Amanda while in Florida. And don't even think about sending me back early!"

"Gary, thank you. If there's anything you guys need, anything at all, know that you can count on me."

"We know. Now I plan to take an hour or so to shop for my little one. Of course I don't know the gender, it's too early for that, but I saw a lot of neutral things on my travels that I want to go pick up."

"Of course, and we're still on for Disney tomorrow, right?"

"Only if you're up to it."

"An adrenaline rush-filled day with sugar and fun? You can't take that away from me! And I want to buy your new family some of my own gifts."

"Cool, well, we're here." I swallowed hard and reached over, touched Gary's hand. Looking at my shoes, I thanked him for everything.

"Don't mention it. This whole fiasco is horrible, but I do plan to use my skills to catch the creep who killed your parents."

Looking him in the eye after removing my hand from his, I was able to tell him I'd see him after class and wished him luck.

The workshops ran as they typically did, but were packed with tons of useful and surprising information. Thankfully, I wasn't treated with any special care and Trevor continued with business as usual, not mentioning our rendezvous from the night before.

It was sad to watch Stephen hand out our final test and announce that we had forty-five minutes to complete it. We would come back tomorrow to pick up the graded exam and our certificate, if we had passed. I was nervous when the exam only took me a half hour to finish, so I reviewed my answers until I saw two others pass theirs in. At that time I packed my things and met Krista standing in the hallway.

"How did you do?"

"I guess we'll see tomorrow. It was interesting, though. I really learned a lot."

"Listen, I don't know what you have planned for tonight or tomorrow but I would really like to meet with you. When are you heading home?"

Sarah Butland

"Gary and I are going to Disney World tomorrow and we're leaving the next morning. Tonight would be best for me. Did you find something?"

Trevor took that moment to leave the classroom and Krista waved off the question. "Tonight at six, then. I'll meet you in the hotel lobby. It might be best if it's just you and me, if Gary and Trevor are OK with that," she said with a knowing smirk.

"Uhh...yeah, they'll be fine and I'll be there." She had me worried, wondering what she had to tell me and what she knew about Trevor and me. I felt bad for leaving Gary alone again, but I promised I'd make it up to him at Disney World. With a couple of hours before supper I decided to see what he was up to and called his cell phone.

"Amanda?"

"Sorry, no, it's Natalie. I'm finished with class and wanted to know how you would like to spend the next couple of hours. I need to meet Krista for dinner at six but I'm free until then."

"I'll pick you up at the conference. I have an idea."

I took a moment to bid farewell to the friends I had made at the conference and promised to stay in touch with a few of them. I made it to the front door just as Gary was pulling up.

"I'm anxious for you to distract me with your plan."

"Bad day?"

"Not at all. We completed the workshops and took a test. I have to go back tomorrow for my grades and certificate, but other than that, the day is ours."

"Sounds great. I thought we'd go on a little shopping spree right now. I found this incredible store I think you and Amanda would love. I found a few things I think she'll like but I want your opinion."

"You don't mind shopping?"

"Usually I do, but I'm in a good mood. How does that sound?"

"Sounds great! I want to get out of these clothes and find some better ones for tomorrow. Let's go!"

We were already on our way and pulling into the parking lot of the biggest mall I'd ever seen. I had no idea what store Gary had chosen, so I blindly followed his lead. As soon as we entered the store, I was in awe. I couldn't believe the styles, the selection, and the prices, and was so thankful Gary had found the place.

I was so thrilled I didn't even notice how sore my feet were from being in the pumps I had chosen to wear or how uncomfortable I felt in a skirt. We left with bags evenly divided between clothes for myself and Amanda. I knew we'd be sharing everything anyway, but made sure to buy things Amanda would love.

Back at the hotel and with a half hour to spare before meeting Krista, I modeled some of the clothes while Gary helped me pick outfits for that night and for our day at Disney. I couldn't believe my luck. I had chosen him to spend the week with me despite my suspicions and he was taking it so well.

I waited in the lobby for only four minutes before Krista approached and walked with me to her car. She mentioned where she was taking me, ensuring I liked seafood before assuring me the place had the best lobster in town. I was delighted but still uneasy.

The restaurant wasn't far away, for which I was thankful, because I was too nervous to ask what this supper was really about. Krista seemed so caught up in something that she couldn't talk. It wasn't until we placed our order and the waiter left us alone that she broke the news.

"The fingerprints didn't provide us anything. I checked them against everything we have, but with no luck. I had them sent to your local police station, to the detective you named. I haven't heard back yet, but that's not surprising."

"I'll just have to keep looking, then. But you could have told me this after class, you certainly don't have to wine and dine me to share this news. You had me terrified!"

"That's not all. The reason I asked you out to dinner is because I have a plan. I don't want to impose and I want you to think about it." Krista reached into her purse and produced a familiar looking paper: my test.

Chapter 31

"Why do you have my test? I thought Stephen was only correcting them tonight."

"He's correcting the others tonight. Yours took priority, and we weren't disappointed. Natalie, you're the first to score a hundred percent on this test — ever! — and I suspect, the only one who will from your class. We set the questions up with errors to catch those not paying attention, but you went back and fixed every one so that you could correctly answer them."

My face burned. I didn't know what to say. I was amazed, shocked, surprised, impressed, confused. "What does this mean?"

"That part is up to you. Stephen and I discussed this possibility yesterday but didn't really take it seriously until now. We want to contact the school here to see about getting you transferred."

"To Florida? I have family back home. They may be buried underground, but they are still present in my life."

"Your parents will be with you wherever you go, Natalie. You have friends — good friends — and I don't want to diminish those relationships, but you need to realize what an opportunity this is. You'd continue working closely with Stephen and me while you finish school. Then you'd intern with us and start your career, going out in the field with us whenever necessary."

"I'm speechless..."

"Good. It's a lot to think about and I don't want to hear any of your off-the-cuff excuses. I want you to seriously consider this. You're one-of-a-kind, Natalie. Criminals need to watch out for you."

"But I can't even track down my own stalker...or my parents' murderer."

"Listen, we want to continue helping you with that, too. Stephen and I need to stay here next week to wrap things up, but we plan to come to Boston to work with Detective Brock to get this guy. It's the least we can do for you."

"But I haven't said I'd transfer yet."

"Your decision has nothing to do with us helping out. Once we start a case, we need to finish it, especially when it involves a friend. You need to know you're not alone in this."

The lobster was delicious and the side dishes just as scrumptious. The conversation left me a lot to think about. I felt terrible eating the meal in such silence, but Krista didn't seem to mind. My head was spinning and it didn't need any wine this time.

When we were leaving, Krista told me to come by tomorrow to pick up my certificate; telling others my exam grade would be entirely up to me. I told her I'd be there at eight in the morning to make sure I still had the full day with Gary at Disney. "Thank you very much, Krista. And I'll thank Stephen tomorrow. When do I need to tell you my decision?"

"Take your time. There's not much of this semester left, if you want to finish that in Boston. We haven't had a chance to talk to the Dean here yet to see if this is even possible, but we will before you make your decision. I'm sure he'd be delighted to have you and make room for you to take whatever classes you want. And, of course, don't worry about tuition, here or in Boston. You're an investment — we have you covered."

This news thrilled me beyond compare. I had scholarships already but not enough to cover every year. I couldn't believe what I was hearing.

Krista drove me back to the hotel in a completely different silence than before. I didn't know how to keep my excitement from Gary but knew I had to until I decided or talked to Amanda. Krista hugged me when she dropped me off, confirming that I'd be there tomorrow to pick up my certificate.

Gary was already asleep when I got back to our room. I looked at the bedside clock to find it was later than I'd thought. I also knew he'd want to be well rested for the day. I crept to the bedside table to see what time he had set the alarm for and saw it was already set for 6:30 a.m. This would give me plenty of time to get ready and be at the school at 8:00 a.m.

I changed and crawled into bed, too excited to sleep or worry about Gary's sexual advancements and too terrified to embrace the moment's full potential. I finally slept and had mixed feelings about the alarm sounding. Reaching to press snooze, I saw Gary, showered and dressed, already sitting on the edge of the bed.

"Good morning, Natalie. Is it too early for you?"

"No, it's fine. I promised Krista I'd be at the school at eight. I just didn't sleep well, must be from all the excitement." I smiled knowingly.

"I didn't figure I'd sleep well, either. I was in bed at eight last night and fell asleep pretty quickly. I talked to Amanda, too. She is excited to have us come home tomorrow."

"I bet. She must be bored. Do you want to go out for breakfast, or order something up?"

"Breakfast is already on its way. French toast with strawberries and whipped cream OK?"

"Sounds delicious. I'll just get in the shower and be right out."

In the shower, the extent of the opportunity Krista and Stephen had offered me hit me even harder than it had the night before. At one of the best schools in the world, the most prestigious people in the field wanted to work with me! As the hot

147

water hit my skin I trembled, concerned with how everyone would react when I told them I needed to take this opportunity. I felt I was being selfish, deciding so quickly, but I knew it was stupid of me to think of passing the opportunity up.

I knew Professor Matthews would be so impressed but also disappointed that he was going to lose me. I also understood that this meant moving away from my parents and all that I was. Growing up was difficult. Although I knew *what* I wanted to be in life, I had never thought about *where* I wanted to be.

Hearing breakfast arrive, I hurried, putting on the clothes I had previously chosen for the day. Looking in the mirror, I saw that I was positively glowing and knew it wasn't from the Florida sun. Gary was waiting and the smell of maple syrup made me sit down quickly. When we finished eating, we packed some things for the day and hurried out the door. On the way, I told him that I'd appreciate him going into the school with me and thought it would be another great opportunity for him to talk with Stephen and Krista.

"I invited them to spend the day with us but they have to be at the school until all the students have shown."

"I'd love to see them again but I am kind of glad they aren't able to come. Today's about fun, not work, and if they were with us I'd be too focused on asking questions than about enjoying the rides."

"I agree."

We arrived to a nearly empty parking lot and walked into the school to see only Stephen and Krista. I crossed my fingers that they wouldn't allude to anything we had discussed previously. "Natalie, you're early!"

"I hope that's OK. If you're not ready we can come back."

"It's perfectly OK. Hi, Gary. I hear you have a jam-packed day ahead of you."

"I can't wait."

"We'll be sure not to keep you, then. Here's your certificate, Natalie," Stephen held out his hand with an official-looking document. "Be sure to show this to your professor in Boston."

"I'll get it framed as soon as I get back home and bring it to school immediately. Everyone will be so jealous!"

"As well they should be."

Gary grinned and admitted he had been jealous when I had merely been chosen to attend. Now he was beyond admiration at seeing my certificate.

"Will I be seeing you again?"

"Sooner than you think, Gary. We're going to visit Boston really soon. We have talks lined up and hope you'll be attending."

"Awesome! Front row and center, with Natalie by my side!"

Everyone hugged each other and we were off, running into Trevor on the way out. "How did you do?"

"Better than expected. Are you nervous?"

"Nah...I usually do OK, but I hate the pressure of tests. Put me out in the field and I'm a natural. Make me write about it and I choke. Hi, Gary. Any plans for today?"

I was nervous that Trevor would invite himself along but didn't stop Gary from answering.

"Oh, I wish I could join you but I'm heading back home at noon, which is the only reason I'm here so early. I better not keep you. I'm anxious to get my results, so I'll say farewell now."

"Gary, I'll meet you out in the car, OK?"

"Sure, I'll pull around front."

"Trevor, I'm sorry we didn't get to talk about the other night."

"What, oh the dinner?" he teased.

"I just..."

"No need to explain. It's usually the man who needs to backpedal —"

"Oh, so you've done this before? I should have known." I was horrified and then realized I wanted more than a one-night stand. I wanted to see where this would go; I was curious, but none of that mattered. I couldn't be with someone who was so casual about sex.

"No, Natalie. You were my first...sorry, my first impulsive...sorry, I don't know how to say this."

"Don't worry, neither do I. I want to see you again. I'll need to call on you at some point when I'm out in the field!" We exchanged contact information and promised to stay in touch, one promise I knew I'd keep. We hugged, we kissed, we said our goodbyes, and then I was on my way to Disney and Trevor was on his way home. On the way to the theme park, Gary asked about my test score.

"I was hoping you wouldn't ask," I was relived he didn't mention Trevor, "And am glad you waited until now. I got a hundred percent!" I didn't tell him that I was the first student to score perfectly; that bit of information would come out in Boston.

I didn't want to pay for a day at Disney World just to follow the kids around so when they parked, I turned around and headed to the airport. I'd meet them back in Boston.

Gary couldn't get over my brilliance and kept congratulating me until we had our theme park maps in hand and were focused on choosing what to do first. With only one day at Disney, we knew we'd have to plan well and just have fun with it.

After a wonderful day filled with sugary treats and ice cold drinks, we didn't want to leave. By 9:00 p.m. our feet were sore, we had ridden the rides we wanted to go on most, and had seen the sights we wanted to see, so we headed back to the hotel. I didn't once consider the idea of being followed or the problems that were ahead; I relaxed completely for the first time in a very long time.

We slept like hibernating bears that night but immediately awoke when we heard the alarm sound. Although we'd had a wonderful time, neither of us could wait to get home.

Gary didn't even think to take any medication for the plane ride as he eagerly chatted about the day before and what was waiting for him in Boston. I couldn't help but think about the decision I had to make while he talked about his own life changing. It took me a second to realize what was happening when he pulled out an engagement ring he had bought.

"Gary?"

"Do you think she'll like it?"

"Oh...yes, I do. I just wonder if now is the right time to ask her. I'm sure she doesn't want you thinking about marrying her only because she's having your child."

"That's definitely not the case...I've been looking so hard for the perfect ring and found it the day before she told me the news. I was so stressed about being away from her so much before we left — I wanted to find just the right ring."

That explained his earlier odd behavior. *Thank goodness*! I thought. "I know and she knows that too, but the timing might not be the best right now."

"You're right, I just...everything is happening just like I always imagined. I love her to pieces and can't imagine my life without her. I realized this while being away from her these last few days. She's my everything"

"And you are hers. You'll see that, but I would suggest waiting until you are convinced she wouldn't think this is a spontaneous proposal. Make sure she knows you want to marry *her*, not the mother of your child."

As he thanked me, he put the ring back in his pocket and the pilot announced our imminent landing. We arrived safely and happily and I drove Gary home, considering whether to stop in at

Sarah Butland

the police station for a quick update on my case. I decided
Detective Brock would call me soon enough, so I drove past the
station without stopping.

I left the couple to celebrate their togetherness, and then
drove home and cautiously entered my apartment. Happy to see
my cat, I dumped my bags at the front door and made my way to
bed. I collapsed without changing as thoughts of the conference
ran through my head until I finally fell asleep.

My ringing phone finally woke me and I answered it
groggily.

Chapter 32

"Natalie, you're home! How did it go?"

"Professor, I owe you so much. It was fantastic and I have a lot to talk to you about. They want me to transfer."

"Who does? Transfer where?"

I guess I wasn't the only one feeling a bit overwhelmed. "Stephen and Krista. To Florida University. They are coming to Boston and I want you to meet them. You haven't yet, have you?"

"No, I haven't. They, of course, weren't the ones teaching when I attended the conference. I can't wait to meet them and discuss their taking you away. I'd hate to see you go, but I understand that it might be the best thing for your career."

"I haven't decided yet. I have to talk things over with you, my friends, and Stephen and Krista again. I'm finishing this term here anyway and then who knows."

"Very exciting for you, Natalie. Now, back to business. We do have a final press conference lined up for you. The reporters wanted to have it tomorrow but I thought it best for you to get settled first. Don't worry about coming to school in the morning, just relax and prepare. Unfortunately I was only able to put it off until Tuesday afternoon, so we'll meet everyone in the auditorium again right after our class. If you'd like, we can go out to supper tomorrow to review everything."

I hesitated only for a second before agreeing to do just that. I didn't want to take him away from his family any more than I already had, but this seemed like a necessary meeting. "Thanks again Professor Ma—"

"Brian. And no problem, I'm glad to help a truly ambitious student achieve her dreams."

"Thanks, good night."

After hanging up the phone, I fell back to sleep but was interrupted again; this time it was Amanda calling. "Natalie, I'm getting married! You'll be my maid of honor, of course. I couldn't imagine you not being there with me. Can you believe it? I need to come over to show you my ring. It's gorgeous!"

"Congratulations, girl! This is very exciting news, and of course I'd be thrilled to be your maid of honor. Just don't pick out a nasty dress for me. I need to find someone too, you know."

"I do and I was thinking..."

"Stop there. This is one aspect in my life that doesn't need your meddling," I said with the best of intentions. "Celebration dinner, Tuesday night after I meet with the reporters for the final time. I'll have some news, too!"

"Really? Tell me now. Did you meet someone?"

"I met a lot of people, and I need sleep right now so I don't want to get into it. I may not be at school tomorrow. Gary doesn't need to go either, but I'm going to try to be there. If you don't see me tomorrow you'll see me on Tuesday for sure. Gotta sleep..."

"Good night, sleep well, Natalie. I'm SO excited!"

She actually took my putting her off a lot better than I could have imagined. I was thrilled for her and Gary but did need to go back to sleep, which didn't take me long. I fell into a deep sleep only minutes after unplugging the phone and slept until nine Monday morning.

After showering, dressing, and eating, I decided to make it to my afternoon classes to get back some normalcy in my life. I wasn't out to impress anyone, but knew Professor Matthews would be impressed no matter how skillfully I shrugged off my presence. Surprising myself, I stayed pretty focused and only thought of the impending dinner date at the end of the day.

Professor Matthews and I agreed to meet at the main entrance to the school immediately after class and drive to the restaurant in one car. I was too excited to care about what the watching students thought or said; my future was in my hands and I was grabbing hold.

Brian told me right away that, even though the school and he would miss me, it didn't make sense for me to pass up the opportunity I had been presented. "I know, I just...my parents' graves are here and I visit them often."

"Understandable, but I do know you'll be back. Your schooling will just be a few more years, interning will be another couple, and then you'll be back. I have no doubt where your heart is and I know that you'll be better prepared to solve your parents' case when you have a clear head."

"How did you know about my parents? I never told you about that."

"Natalie, I had to do a quick background check before sending you to the conference. I'm sorry I didn't tell you earlier. I wouldn't be able to let go either if my parents were murdered, God forbid. You can't be blamed for trying to solve this case, but I think, and don't tell my boss, that your classes and mentoring in Florida will be much better for you."

I was a bit put off but decided I should have told him about my parents anyway, so I let it go. "It's a lot to think about, Brian, even though I've already made up my mind."

"I hope you're not letting this opportunity go to waste. Something this big probably won't come again."

"I know...we're here. And promise me, no wine tonight. I'm celebrating sober and taking in your infinite wisdom."

"I don't know about that — the wisdom, that is. No wine though, promise. But Natalie, I am going to have a beer and hope that you'll join me for that at least."

"One beer? Deal."

Dinner was delightful and the professor was filled with a lot of advice for me, but even he couldn't prepare me for everything the final press conference had to offer.

Chapter 33

As Professor Matthews prepped me for the press conference the next morning, I saw Krista enter the auditorium and it wasn't long before I saw Stephen behind her. "What are you guys doing here?"

"I told you we were coming to Boston. We were here yesterday but heard the press conference was postponed so you could rest, so we thought we'd lie low."

"Stephen, Krista. I hope you slept well last night."

"Professor Matthews, you knew?"

"I deduced they'd be following you and found them registered at the Marriott. They made me promise not to mention it to you. Are you surprised?"

"Surprised? I'm amazed, honored, yes, and surprised! How long will you be staying in town?"

"All week. We need your decision before we leave so we can prepare everything with the school for next year."

"Wow, that's quick. Just to clarify, you actually mean next calendar year?"

"After Christmas break you'd be attending Florida University if you so choose. Classes start January fourth so we could move you down on the second, giving you time to celebrate the New Year with your friends here."

"If I tell you my decision early, will you leave Boston earlier, or are you still staying for the full week?"

"We are lecturing tomorrow and Thursday, which you're invited to either way, and are leaving Friday morning no matter what you decide."

"I'll go."

"Excuse me?" everyone was surprised, even me.

"Professor Matthews, you're right. I can't pass up this opportunity and I really have no ties here save for my parents and Amanda. But, as you said, I'll be back, and we all know my parents aren't going anywhere. Krista and Stephen, you've inspired me and helped me so much already that I know it'll only do wonders to continue working with you. Now, you'll have to excuse me, I have an interview with local reporters."

There weren't any inconsiderate questions at this press conference, or maybe I was just in a much better mood to handle them. Either way, the time flew by and I had little time to think about my stalker, even though I was being stared at the entire afternoon.

Overhearing her decision to move to Florida in two months, I grimaced. I didn't want to move again, but didn't know if I could trust her to not continue working on her parents' case. Although she wouldn't have the Boston contacts anymore, I knew that she would have excellent help in Florida. I'd have to keep a much closer eye on her until the end of December and then decide. She was turning into too much trouble and I often wondered if my freedom was even worth it.

It certainly didn't feel as if I was free now, with having to keep tabs on her. Figuring I had gotten this far, I may as well keep trying for my freedom. I was so addicted now I couldn't imagine my life without her.

Chapter 34

Although Krista and Stephen invited me to dinner after the press conference, I had to decline because the night was for Amanda and me. As a rain check, we planned for dinner Wednesday after their lectures.

After the press conference, I returned to my apartment more nervous about my impending dinner date than I had been about the press conference itself. I was never nervous about meeting with my best friend, but knowing tonight was a momentous occasion I couldn't help but worry. As I was dressing down, my phone rang; it was Amanda.

"All set?"

"Just about. Actually, by the time you get here I'll be ready, if you want to go together. Or, if you give me fifteen minutes, I can pick you up," I offered.

"I just plan to have one glass of wine with you — don't worry, the doctor said it was OK this early on. You know I wouldn't do anything to harm my little one. And I'll be OK to drive. I'll leave right now and pick you up."

"Sounds great, don't bother coming up. I'll just meet you at your car. And, Amanda, congratulations again on both of your pieces of news!"

We said our goodbyes and I took a very deep breath. I wanted this night to be all about Amanda and Gary, but I also didn't want her hearing about my decision from someone else.

Even though the people who knew of my decision had promised to keep it quiet and I trusted them, I couldn't keep it quiet myself.

After brushing my teeth, grabbing my purse, and taking one last confidence-building breath I headed to the parking lot, where Amanda was waiting.

As I was getting in the car, she turned and showed me her ring. "It's GORgeous! Congrats again," I said as I gave her an awkward car hug.

"Isn't it? But I hear you have something to celebrate, too. Why didn't you tell me?"

I quickly started thinking of excuses, possible ways she could have found out, and reasons to justify my decision when she interrupted, "A hundred percent on your exam? That's amazing — yet not surprising, knowing you."

"Oh..."

"Gary told me before I left. He wanted to make sure I wasn't taking over our celebration with wedding plans. Don't look so...shocked. Is something wrong?"

"No, not at all. I just...yes, I got a perfect score, and made quick friends with both instructors. They are amazing scientists. I'm sorry I didn't tell you earlier."

"You're forgiven. Where to?"

"Your choice. I can personally recommend the Meat and Griddle but I don't think they want me back there. I heard that Fish and Tackle is good. The Tackle refers to any animal you can tackle if you don't feel like seafood. I'm paying so don't you worry about cost."

"Then it's decided. Remind me where that is again."

When we arrived, we were directed to a corner table and ordered two glasses of white wine. We looked over our menu while we waited for our drinks, so we were prepared with our food order and quickly toasted our individual successes when the waiter was off. "I have something else I need to tell you about."

"Something fantastic, I hope."

"Well..." The waiter returned with our food and took our second drink order before I had the chance to continue. The interruption gave me the time I needed for an extra breath before I blurted out my news: "I'm moving to Florida in January."

"Oh my God, why? What about my wedding? What am I going to do? How is this fantastic news?"

"Krista and Stephen got me a full scholarship to attend Florida University. It would be a crucial move for my career to attend and then go on to intern with them. I know it's happening quickly but this is my chance, Amanda. Of course I'll be coming back for your wedding, unless you decide to have it in Florida." The silence that followed was irritating, to say the least, and then Amanda had the nerve to start eating!

"Eat up. Your dinner is getting cold."

"Don't you have anything to say?"

Her sudden enormous smile said it all but she verbalized it anyway. "Natalie, I'm so proud of you," she said as she got up from the table to give me a hug. "Of course I'll miss you terribly but you'd be stupid not to jump on this chance, and I know you're not stupid. Now let's eat, we are celebrating, remember! Oh, and waiter, two more glasses of wine please, this time one without alcohol."

When we began eating and I was able to relax a bit more, I pried, "So, let's talk wedding. Do you have a date yet?"

"We were considering January first. I don't want to waste time because I don't plan to tell my parents I'm pregnant until we're married. You know how much Dad will freak! When I found out that I was pregnant it took everything I had not to tell them, but because we're engaged it will be so much easier. I'm only four weeks in so I figure I can get away with pretending I am early when the baby arrives."

"Sounds great. I know how hard it is to keep the pregnancy from your parents but January is not that far away. I'm so glad I won't have moved yet so I can participate in absolutely everything."

We spent the next hour and a half discussing colors, locations, flowers, reception, very much like an old married couple. Although we couldn't make any decisions without Gary, it was fun to just kick back, forget about all my troubles, and talk girl stuff.

We only mentioned my stalker on the way home, after making arrangements to meet over the weekend to go dress shopping. "Any headway reported by Detective Brock?" Amanda opened.

"I've been putting off calling him but he hasn't called me since I've been back. I really don't know if that's a good thing or not. I'm going to call him when I get home. Has he called Gary yet?"

"No. I'll go upstairs with you then, because I want to know how close Brock is to getting this creep. The one good thing about going to Florida is you'll leave all this behind."

"That's the good AND the bad. Thanks for offering, but you really don't —"

"I know I don't have to, I want to, Natalie," she confirmed as she parked the car. When we got upstairs, I didn't even take my shoes off; I immediately went to the phone and saw there were messages, one of which was from Detective Brock asking me to call him, so I did.

"Thank you for calling me back so quickly. It's important that we meet. When's best for you?"

"That depends, do you have something?"

"Nothing too significant, but intriguing enough for us to further investigate. I'm working from noon till eight tomorrow."

"I can be at the station at four thirty. Is there a way to guarantee you'll be there and not out fighting crime, though?"

"Not at all, just give us a call before heading this way and I'll do my best to be around. See you then."

"Detective Brock, is there anything I should be concerned with?"

"Of course! You do have a stalker but nothing more serious than before you left. Be aware, be safe, and I'll see you tomorrow."

I updated Amanda, who offered to stay the night knowing I was already driving myself frantic with worry, but I told her to go home to her fiancé. *Insisted* she go. I had a lot to think about, to come to grips with, and to do that I wanted to be alone.

Chapter 35

When Amanda left I took off my shoes, found a pair of PJ's, and got in the bath. The water was just about hot enough to dissolve my worries, but I realized it wouldn't be that easy. The stalker was real, not some imagined horrible nightmare I had concocted while away. I tried to concentrate on my upcoming school transfer and all that had to be done before I left Boston, but my mind kept returning to what Detective Brock could possibly need to meet with me about. I was happy to have brought a pad of paper and pen with me to start making a list on what I needed to accomplish, and noticed how quickly the tasks were adding up. It took me a little while to realize I kept adding 'meet with Detective Brock' again and again.

What did make a very important item on my list was to tell my landlord I was moving, because my lease was until the end of the school year. She was pretty understanding, so I hoped we could work something out if I gave her my notice now. I planned to see her first thing in the morning. Once I noticed I was continually adding my meeting with Detective Brock to my list, I decided to drop the list to the floor and relax, letting the glasses of wine finally go to my head.

The bath water became too cold to bear, so I finally got out and went to bed after setting my alarm for a half hour earlier than usual. Knowing that my landlord was an early bird, I easily convinced myself to meet with her before class in the morning.

The next day, I knocked on my landlord's door and waited patiently for her to answer, surprised when a man adorned in only a towel opened the door. "Sorry to disturb you so early, I'm looking for Ms. Stork. Is she awake yet?" I was too busy looking at the man's toes to avoid looking at anything else that I failed to recognize him or to notice Ms. Stork limping to the door.

"Jeffery, who is it?" Ms. Stork voiced from somewhere I couldn't see.

"Natalie Hartman, Apt 3B. If this is a bad time —" Ms. Stork appeared, fortunately appropriately dressed, and the man disappeared into what must have been her kitchen by the sounds and smells that soon came out of it. "I want to speak to you about my lease. If there's a better time..."

"No, no don't be silly. Come sit down," she motioned towards a couch covered in plastic as she took the chair across from it. "What's this about your lease? If I remember correctly, and please forgive me if I don't, the apartment is yours until the end of the year."

"You're right, that's what the original lease was for, but something came up and I want to move out sooner."

"Something wrong with the place, Natalie?"

"Oh no, it's perfect and I'm sure you can have it rented again immediately. I'm transferring to Florida University at the beginning of next year, but I promise to help find someone to move in when I move out."

"Sure, we'll work something out. I'll start advertising now. Are you able to move out if someone needs to move in before January?"

"I can make arrangements, whatever needs to be done."

"Great, now can I get back to my breakfast?"

"Of course, I'm sorry, I just wanted to tell you as soon as possible. If I hear of anyone who wants to move in, you'll be the first to know."

Elated, I went to school with the knowledge that everything was going to work out wonderfully, but halfway through my day I got the eerie feeling that something was wrong. Although I was looking forward to my meeting with Detective Brock after school, I was nervous about what he had to say.

I came to find out there had really been no reason for me to be nervous. Detective Brock had very little for me and only wanted to meet with me to ask questions for which I had no answers. I was stumped, and as I walked out of the police station I knew I had to let the police do their job or take further action. Realizing I should never forget that my life could be in danger, I decided I had to act — and quickly.

Seeing her walk out of the police station with a slight smirk on her face and a more obvious look of determination mixed with focus, I knew I had to act — and quickly. Unfortunately, I had to wait until we were further away from the police station's parking lot.

I followed her back to her apartment building, where I abducted her.

Chapter 36

I had seen someone following me and knew that the person would continue to follow me until I parked my car at home. On my way, I called Detective Brock and informed him of the make, model and license plate of my stalker, proud that I was able to keep a level head and obtain this information. I knew that all the small details would be important and that my life was in much more immediate danger than I thought possible at 21 years of age. I didn't realize I shouldn't have gotten out of my car after arriving at home.

Too soon, my phone was taken from me and someone shoved me into the trunk of the Saturn Ion that, only moments before, I had lost sight of. Feeling I could have easily overpowered my attacker, I decided it safest to allow him to take me and let Detective Brock be the police while I played the victim and followed this line of adventure through.

Closing my eyes, I concentrated on how many turns the car took from my apartment, the conditions of the road, and the distance we drove. This tactic is commonly seen in movies and television shows and is one of the most realistic things they depict. When I had an opportunity to talk to someone, I would have details to provide as to our whereabouts. Thinking about breaking the taillight out with my — naively — unbound hands I second-guessed my actions, believing escape might be more effective once we arrived at our destination.

Before I could make up my mind completely, the car stopped, three left turns, six right turns and about twenty minutes from my apartment. Thinking I'd be left alone for a while — by my determining, we were at the mall — I scrapped the idea of waiting until we were at the final destination. I waited three minutes after hearing the car door slam, then punched through a taillight and began to scream. Unfortunately my timing was off; the only person who came to the car was my abductor, who once again took his place in the driver's seat. Fortunately he hadn't noticed my efforts to be rescued. My tally of turns and time continued.

At the very least I wanted to get one small glimpse of whoever had kidnapped me, but I had to concentrate on the things I did know instead. Not knowing how long I had before my kidnapper decided to physically harm me, I made up my mind to comply as best I could with everything he demanded of me. I was just hoping we'd arrive at our destination soon because I really needed to pee.

While I looked out of the hole I had created with the broken taillight, I continued to count the turns. I was thankful that I thought to keep track because I no longer recognized where we were. In total, I counted twenty-three left and thirty-four right turns before the car finally stopped and the trunk opened.

My abductor was masked, so I concluded that I knew him and was hopeful that I'd remain alive when things were sorted out. He wouldn't even talk; he merely wrote down what I was supposed to do in barely-legible handwriting. Once inside an isolated house, I explained that I needed to use the bathroom and he escorted me down the hall. He left the door open but turned around while I urinated. I was careful when I opened the medicine cabinet a crack, only to find it completely empty. Afterward, I was taken to a windowless attic, made to walk in front of my abductor, and seated in a chair. Hands finally tied and then blindfolded, I was left alone for what seemed like an hour.

When my abductor returned, he removed my blindfold and handed me a note that asked what I knew about my parents' murder. So this WAS connected! Without much hesitation I said I wasn't any closer to finding the culprit than I had been last year, but that I hoped to find something soon.

He didn't like that, but I was making him angry on purpose. I slowed down his thought process by clouding judgment with frustration; I wanted to push some buttons while I tried to fit more pieces together. Watching him write more to the note, I was able to determine he was left-handed, because he was writing horribly with his right. His hands were gloved, possibly because I'd recognize them, but another thought occurred to me: maybe this wasn't a man at all. The gloves could be hiding painted fingernails and slender fingers and might be intended to make the hands seem bulkier.

Looking more carefully at the handwriting when the note was handed back to me, I was even more convinced a female had written it. She was now growing impatient and I needed to read the question instead of trying to analyze the writing: 'Who is helping you?'

"No one, there's no one helping me. My parents' case is cold so I'm on my own." I wanted to tell her that I would stop investigating if she would just let me go, but that would be an obvious lie. I was now even more determined to leave this nightmare behind by solving my parents' case and mine.

The abductor grabbed the paper from my hands, furiously wrote on it again, and then handed it back. This time it read:

'I'm warning you to stop. Your parents' case is not as simple as you think. What you are searching for will end up destroying you.'

Chapter 37

After reading the note, I let the paper drop to the ground, wondering what was behind this statement. My abductor retrieved the paper, wrote on it again, handed to me, and waited for me to respond.

"You have my word. I'll wait here for fifteen minutes and then go." At that, my abductor freed my hands and disappeared quickly. Staying true to my word, I waited until my watch read 9:00 p.m. and then made my way down the attic ladder to the main house after retrieving the paper for possible fingerprints. Even though I knew it had been handled with gloves while I was in the room, I couldn't be sure my abductor had handled it that way the entire time.

I went back to the bathroom and very quickly grabbed a comb I had seen when I was in there earlier. If we found fingerprints on the note that should be enough evidence, but if there were more than one person involved I needed to know.

Too nervous to look around much more, I almost tripped over my cell phone, left on the floor in front of the door. Picking it up, I opened the door and began to run, not sure if my abductor had really left me to live. When I finally ran out of breath, I found Detective Brock on my speed dial and called.

"Charlie, it's Natalie. I need help."

"Natalie, I found information on the car you gave me. Wait, you need my help? What did you find out?"

"Good, but Charlie, I need a ride. I was kidnapped. I'm fine but the stalker took me to an abandoned house. I have so much to tell you. I'm in the middle of nowhere. I can only give you what I remember as directions from my apartment. I counted the turns and the drive took about forty minutes. What I see right now is industrial buildings, nothing but concrete and pavement...wait, I think...no, sorry, none of these buildings have names on them."

"I know where you are, I'll send someone...no, I'll be there as soon as possible. Don't walk far."

"I won't. Thanks, Charlie. I have so much to tell you."

"Tell me when I get there, and Natalie, don't tell anyone else." With that he hung up and I made my way to the closest building and sat against its wall. Thoughts were scurrying through my head like rats in abandoned buildings, but I couldn't put my finger on what had seemed so familiar about my abductor. I was punishing myself for not being able to determine his or her identity when Detective Brock arrived. I told him everything I knew and what I suspected before he even asked.

I asked Detective Brock for evidence bags, retrieved them from his back seat, and bagged the two items I had collected, explaining why I took them and nothing else. When I concluded, I took a deep breath and asked what our next step was.

"I'm amazed you thought to collect evidence. Please bag your cell phone, too, as we can never be too careful. But, Natalie, your next step is to visit a hospital to get checked out —"

"I'm fine."

"I won't take no for an answer. I'm dropping you off at Mass General and I'll call Amanda to pick you up there. In the meantime, I'll come back here and try to find the house you were in. You said it's a two-story with pale yellow siding — it shouldn't be too hard to find out here in the industrial park. Once I've located the address, I'll be able to trace the owner and see if I can get a match to anyone you know."

"Did you figure out who rented the car?"

"Yes, a J. Smith. I assume it's an alias, but I have my people checking for any J. Smiths in the area. Do you happen to know any? The clerk said the person who rented the car was male."

"J...J...for some reason I think the 'J' is familiar but, no, it's gotta be my paranoia."

"If you think of anything, anyone at all, you have to let me know. Don't assume it's nothing, Natalie."

"No, I can't think of anyone." I was still filtering through my acquaintances, someone who would have been around at the time of my parents' murder, when we arrived at the hospital. Detective Brock offered to go in with me, partly to make sure I got checked out, but I promised that I would be fine. He watched me enter the emergency room before driving off.

Everything was physically fine with me and I told Amanda so when she picked me up. "I'm glad you're OK. Now tell me what happened."

I told her everything I had told Detective Brock and then asked, "Do you have any idea who my abductor could be?"

"I'm sorry, really sorry but I don't. This just doesn't make sense, any of it. Who would want to hurt you?"

"That's just it...the abductor seemed very careful not to hurt me at all. It was almost as if they intended for me to walk away unharmed, but that's ridiculous. They must know I won't leave my parents' case alone."

"You're staying with Gary and me. I won't take no for an answer and I'm not leaving you alone anymore. Not until this is figured out and that creep is behind bars."

I was thankful and relieved that Amanda somehow knew I wanted to stay with her but hadn't made me ask. Everything was happening so quickly now that I couldn't think straight. And then something so obvious came to me that I should have noticed before. "Oh my God..."

"What is it?"

"The stuffed animal, it was...no, it can't be..."

"What, Natalie? Should I call Charlie?"

"The stuffed animal that someone pushed through the cat door, I can't be certain — no, I *am* certain — it was the same stuffed animal my mother and father gave me my first Christmas. The only difference was that mine has a Baby's First Christmas collar, but everything else was the same. How did my stalker know about that?"

Chapter 38

"Do you still have the stuffed animal your parents gave you?"

"Of course, it's right on top of my bookshelf in my bedroom."

"We need to get it to give it to Charlie. It might be important."

"I can't go back there. I won't do it. Let me call Charlie to see if he really will need it."

He did. He thought he could narrow down the search by tracing the stuffed animal back to the stores that carried it. "But I can't..."

"I'll come get your keys and get it myself. Don't worry, you won't need to do anything you don't feel comfortable with. I'm on my way back to the station but I'll swing by Amanda's to pick your keys up. What's her address?"

I gave the detective Amanda's address just as she and I were pulling into her driveway. I asked Amanda about clothes and she promised to let me borrow some of hers for the time being. When we got inside the house I hugged her, thanked her for all she was doing, and then crashed onto her couch. "Let's watch a movie," Amanda suggested.

"Sounds good to me, but if you and Gary were going to go out, don't let me stop you."

"You're crazy, we have our lifetime to go out, and besides, I want to watch a movie with you. It's our tradition on sleepovers. I even have the perfect one —"

"*Beetlejuice!*" we both shrieked. When I was young, my parents wouldn't let me watch any movies above a G-rating, so I'd have to go to Amanda's to watch anything good. We waited until after Charlie picked up my keys to get the party started.

"I just have to call Krista to explain my absence. We were supposed to go out to dinner, but I guess the universe had other plans for me. I'll need to go out with her tomorrow night, but I'm sure she and Stephen won't mind if you come with us."

"That's OK, I will politely decline. You have fun. I'd be bored, anyway."

"Are you sure? I'm sure Krista and Stephen would love to meet you." Amanda insisted she'd be fine and used homework as an excuse to bail.

I dialed Krista's number. "Krista, I'm glad I caught you. I'm very sorry about standing you up, I..."

"No problem, we missed you but we know what it's like to be a student. Homework caught up to you?"

"Not exactly. I was kidnapped. I'm fine, I'm at my friend's house. I have Detective Brock checking into it."

"We have to get this guy, Natalie. Can we meet tomorrow night? Stephen and I will do everything in our power to get him before we have to leave Boston."

I confirmed that we would meet and that I was fine. Then Amanda and I had a blast; the only difference from our previous *Beetlejuice* parties was the alcoholic beverages Amanda gave me to empty her shelves. Gary had agreed to be sober with her for the pregnancy, so I was their alcohol disposal. I didn't mind; the drinks let me forget, even for a little while, the outside world.

When Detective Brock called the next morning, I sobered instantly. He had a lead. "The house is currently owned by the city, but they bought it from a Mr. and Mrs. Richard Stork, who died twenty years ago." He cut short when he heard my small gasp.

"My landlord's last name is Stork but it's got to be a coincidence, although a pretty strange one. She'd be about my parents' age if they were alive. It must just be a coincidence..."

"I'll need to go talk to her —"

"NO! She's being so great with me breaking my lease. I don't want her to think she's a suspect yet. Let me go back and talk to her, maybe something will be familiar to me when I do."

"I'll go with you. You're not doing it alone," I heard Amanda say over my shoulder.

I covered the handset and spoke to Amanda, "But you have class. I'm missing much more than I should be, but I have a good excuse. You don't."

"I'll be fine. Let me worry about my classes. You have too much on your plate already."

"Detective Brock? Sorry about that. Amanda will come with me," I volunteered. "I'll pretend she's the one who wants the apartment."

"OK, but don't do anything rash. You're just there for information, and not much of it. Let me do the detecting, Natalie. I don't want you harmed in any way." I thought he was kind to say that; it felt like more than a policeman's advice, but I didn't think I had much to worry about. It seemed whoever was after me wanted me alive and well, just that I stop looking into my parents' murder. They'd have to kill me before I stopped investigating, but I didn't want to push my luck with whoever it was.

I called Ms. Stork in advance this time, not wanting to catch her at a bad time. The voicemail picked up so I left a message asking her to call me back and explained that I had someone interested in renting my place. Just after I told Amanda my plan, Ms. Stork returned my call and said she was at home.

Nervous that Ms. Stork would recognize Amanda as a regular visitor to my place, I asked her to dress down. I didn't think my landlord had ever seen Amanda, but I took every precaution I could imagine. I was also going to have Amanda drop me off at the apartment and arrive a few minutes later because I didn't believe Ms. Stork knew I wasn't staying there now.

When we arrived, I went upstairs to tidy up my place a bit while Amanda met with Ms. Stork. I was putting away the last dish when they knocked on my door. Not wanting to be too obvious, I simply said, "It's so nice to meet you officially, Amanda. I've seen you in class but never had the chance to talk. Come in, it's a very nice place."

Amanda knew where everything was, of course, but let the landlord lead her through while I observed. Nothing Ms. Stork did or said convinced me that she was anything but my landlord, so I was finally relieved when they were through looking and I could be myself once again. Meeting Amanda back at her car, I called Detective Brock and explained my lack of findings to him while Amanda listened in.

She was so naive and too oblivious to understand I knew what they were up to. I took a few acting classes myself when I was younger and knew just how to stay hidden in view of the peering eye.

I also knew that Natalie was not giving up and that, if necessary, I would follow her to Florida. It wouldn't take much for me to consider it necessary.

Chapter 39

From Amanda's house, I checked my messages and was delighted to hear Krista's voice reconfirming our plans to meet. I called her back immediately and we decided on a restaurant and time. I arrived fifteen minutes early and ordered a pitcher of beer for the table.

I was surprised to see Professor Matthews arrive next. He explained that Krista and Stephen had thought it would be OK for him to join us. I hesitated slightly, not aware of how much Krista and Stephen had shared with my professor thus far, and I was happy to see them walk in while Brian was taking his seat.

To Brian's apology for the surprise, I said, "No, it's fine. I'm glad they invited you. Please excuse me for a minute." I met my other dinner guests out of Brian's earshot and asked if they had told him anything about my stalker yet.

"No, of course not, but we checked him out and know that he's not your stalker."

"That's not what I meant but..." I suddenly realized exactly why I wasn't sharing my stalker situation with him. Having a crush on a teacher certainly didn't make him innocent, but I was relieved to hear he was cleared. "Sorry, I...I'm glad he checked out and appreciate you doing that for me. I guess it's OK to get his input on this, then. Have you asked him about hiring the driver in Florida yet? I never even thought of that until now."

"We have. Unfortunately he didn't hire Dana either, so we're investigating that. And, Natalie, just because he's innocent doesn't mean he can be fully trusted. It's entirely up to you how much you tell him," Stephen advised.

"Well, I do want to discuss this tonight. I trust your judgment completely, so let's be open about everything."

"Are you sure?" Krista asked.

"I think so. Let's go. If we keep him waiting, he'll be very suspicious."

At the table, we didn't wait long for the waiter to take our orders and place them with the kitchen. I took the opportunity to confess to my professor, "I'm being stalked."

"What?"

"It's been going on a couple of weeks now. Krista and Stephen know all about it and are helping me catch the creep. I wasn't at their lecture today because I was kidnapped last night. Don't worry, I'm fine."

The discussion continued from there until the waiter returned with our food and another pitcher of beer. The night went smoothly and every one of my guests promised to help capture my stalker and help solve my parents' murder. They couldn't spend much time on it but would focus every spare moment on ensuring my safety. I promised to keep them updated on what I learned and what Detective Brock was able to uncover.

"This creep should be worried, if he isn't already."

"That's just it though, I'm not even sure it's a guy. I mean, when I was captured I could have easily overpowered whoever put me in the trunk. And maybe I should end my investigation, but who knows what questions I'd still have. Knowing that this person is aware of my parents' murder has me even more intrigued."

The waiter returned. "Anyone for dessert?"

We all ordered and changed the topic of conversation to thoughts much lighter, although our minds wouldn't easily switch gears.

This girl was costing me a fortune, but the food was amazing. I knew I'd have to lay off my watchful eye and take a breather for a while. Moving on and letting her live her own life was just proving to be more difficult than I'd imagined. Watching someone for twenty years was not only addictive but was now a touch soothing. Getting caught, however, was not my best option.

I asked for my check and left long before Natalie and her friends. Arriving at home, I confessed my whereabouts to Jeffery and asked for his help, not only to keep me away from Natalie but also to keep tabs on her and keep me updated.

Jeffery was such a dear and told me he would help without need for justification. I couldn't ever let him find out what I was up to; he'd leave me in an instant. He was such an innocent darling.

As we were going our separate ways, I confessed to Professor Matthews that I planned to stay home from school again the next day. He told me that it was OK, that he'd tell all of my teachers and bring the class assignments to Amanda's house so I wouldn't fall behind.

Krista and Stephen said their farewells and offered to come back in December to help me move.

"That won't be necessary but I appreciate the offer. I've already taken up way too much of your time and I feel terrible for doing so."

"Don't be ridiculous. Investigating crime is our job — when we're not teaching, that is — and although your case is currently out of our normal jurisdiction we want to ensure the stalker doesn't follow you when you move."

"Thanks again, for everything. You can't possibly know how grateful I am for all of your help. I never thought *I* would be a case to solve, but I suppose no one ever thinks it'll happen to him or her. I trust you'll have a safe trip and I will be in touch."

"As will we. If you hear anything or make sense of even the smallest detail, please call me." Krista hugged me, with an extra tight squeeze and then went to her car with Stephen. Professor Matthews offered to drive me home, not wanting me to wait alone for Amanda to pick me up. I declined, so he insisted on staying until she arrived. I decided to tread where I never had before with him.

"I didn't realize you were married."

"Three years next month. Why do you ask?"

"Just making conversation. When I called your house a while ago, your daughter answered and I was surprised to hear you had a daughter as well."

"My one and only. She's turning thirteen next month and I couldn't be more proud." He left me speechless; I thought a proud father would tell the world about his child but he seemed to be keeping it quiet. "I know what you're thinking: I don't talk about her enough. I feel my professional life and personal life should be kept separate. You'll understand, I'm sure, once you're working out in the field. I don't even carry pictures of my wife and daughter with me, and it kills me. I just can't imagine someone getting to me through them."

"I understand now. I'm just surprised you're so secretive is all. Oh, there's Amanda. And don't worry, Brian, your family is safe with me."

"Be safe, Natalie. If you need anything at all, just call me. Don't worry about waking my family, they'll understand completely."

"Thank you, Brian. It seems I've been saying that a lot but I don't believe I can ever say it enough for what you've done for me. It's been a long day for me so I should get going. You have my cell number if you think of anything."

"I do. Good night, Natalie, be safe."

The drive back to Amanda's was filled with light conversation, but I did confess that Professor Matthews was helping me catch my stalker, and asked Amanda not to tell Gary that the professor was taking such an interest in my case. Trusting her completely, I felt confident that anything shared between us would stay between us.

As soon as we arrived at Amanda and Gary's, I prepared the couch and went to sleep. I slept well into the next day and woke up to an empty house. I saw a note on the fridge from Amanda saying she had to go into school for the morning but would be back in the afternoon. Looking at my watch, I expected her to arrive any moment and held off getting in the shower until she was home.

Before the door opened I listened to three messages left on my home voicemail; Krista, Detective Brock and Professor Matthews had all called with information. I just couldn't believe what was taking shape with my case or how it made any sense. When I hung up the phone, I heard a car pull in the driveway and someone walk up the steps and was nervous it was someone other than Amanda. Fortunately, it was Amanda and I immediately ran to her.

Deciding it best to think things through before voicing my conclusions, I told Amanda I was getting in the shower and then I'd make her lunch. Instead she told me she'd make lunch while I showered, so I escaped to the bathroom.

Turning the water on as hot as my skin could stand, I undressed and got in, all the while trying to come to some other conclusion than my first. I mentally rewound to Professor Matthews' message first, which seemed the most random of the three, and then to Detective Brocks' message: "The initial 'J' stands for Jeffery. Jeffery Smith. Let me know if this means anything."

Chapter 40

The only Jeffery who came to mind was the one who had been at Ms. Stork's place when I went to tell her I would be moving out. I didn't know his last name, didn't know anything about him, but that was where Krista's information came in. She had called to tell me of a link she and Stephen found to my parents' murder. "Natalie, this may be small or nothing at all but I wanted to make sure you heard this from me. A few years ago someone by the name of Olive Stork followed your parents' case very closely. She was a reporter for *The Boston Globe* and wrote extensive articles on your parents' case. You may want to get in touch with her to find out if she learned anything the paper didn't print."

My shower didn't help me figure out how to proceed with all of this information, but I did decide to share it with Amanda over lunch. "She's been your landlord this whole time and didn't say anything? What has she been hiding, and what did Professor Matthews say?"

"I can't believe she hasn't said anything or asked any questions, for that matter. You don't think she's oblivious to the fact that I'm their daughter, do you?"

"It's possible your parents were just another story to her, but there are too many coincidences building up."

"Oh, Brian wants to meet me at the Arm Farm, because he found out something about my mother."

"At the Arm Farm?" And then it dawned on me.

"Oh my God, my mother. She donated her body to science. Maybe her arm ended up there. I have to call him back. I have to meet with him right away. I always knew my mother donated her body to science but I never realized, never fathomed her body could be so close. But I can't jump to conclusions, let me call him."

"Shouldn't you call Detective Brock back first? He needs to know about Stork and Jeffery."

"I'll call him right after. I need to know if my mother's arm is or was at the Arm Farm."

Tears fell as Brian confirmed my suspicions. Although the chances of finding my mother's arm or it even being remotely in a condition to help with the case were almost nil, the knowledge that it was at the Arm Farm was reassuring. We arranged to meet in an hour and then I called Detective Brock to tell him everything I had learned.

"This is all coming together, Natalie. I'm hoping to get the DNA and fingerprint results tomorrow but maybe if you can get some more samples from your landlord and this Jeffery fellow I can match them today. Do not put yourself in any danger, though. Your safety is the most important."

"I know. I have to meet with Professor Matthews first, and depending on how long I am there I may be able to visit Ms. Stork afterwards. I'll try my best to get both hair and fingerprints for you without her knowing. I'll call you back tonight either way."

"Thanks, Natalie. We're getting close, I just know it."

"It just doesn't make sense. Why would someone murder my parents and then stay so near to me?"

"We have too many questions right now and not enough answers, but soon we'll know and you'll be able to put your mind at ease."

"I hope so. I'll call you later, Charlie."

Amanda went with me to the Arm Farm although she felt nauseous at even the idea of being around cadavers. I tried to convince her to stay home or to go to class, but she refused.

As always, Brian was waiting. When Amanda and I approached, he was deep in thought while looking at some papers. He heard us arrive and told us to follow him, explaining that he was looking at a map of which arm once belonged to which individual. It was all kind of creepy, even for me. He kept all names anonymous except for my mother's.

When he stopped we came close to colliding, but Brian didn't seem to notice. "Here," he said as he pointed to some soil. I bent down where he directed and saw a small pile of bones lying under only a thin layer of soil.

"It looks as if it has been tampered with recently. Look at the way the dirt is kicked over it. It seems the mud is deliberately pushed around it, like someone was trying to hide their boot prints. Do you have a schedule of who visited the farm in the past couple of weeks?"

"Not with me, but I can get one — at least of the people who attend our school. There may be others who come here that I won't know about. The Arm Farm is only open to police officers and schools, though it's a very easy location to find and trespass. I'll do what I can to find out who's been here as soon as we get back to school. Do you think there's anything here that will help?"

"I'm not sure. Are we able to take everything back to the school to check?"

"Normally it's not allowed to take evidence off the property, but this could be important to an ongoing investigation so the exception has been made. You should cut a bit around the area, too, in case the last person who inspected it left something behind."

"I'm on it. Wow, I can't believe this used to be my mother's arm so long ago." Most of the arm's bones were still there, which was surprising. When we got my mother's arm back to the school, I left Professor Matthews to inspect it, figuring I'd be an emotional wreck if I tried. I determined we had just enough time for Amanda to visit Ms. Stork and try to get the DNA I needed for comparison. I waited anxiously in the car while Amanda went into the building.

Fortunately she returned with a comb that came with several strands of hair, although the handle wasn't wide enough to bother dusting for prints. I put the comb in one of my evidence bags and asked Amanda to go immediately to the police station, where we met with Detective Brock.

While we waited, the detective compared our new piece of evidence with the piece of hair he already had from my adventures of being kidnapped, and it — preliminarily — was a match. Trying to catch my breath, I sat down on the closest chair and eventually asked Charlie what the next step was.

"I'm sending someone out right now to bring Ms. Stork in for questioning. Obviously she's part of this and we need to figure out how."

"What if she's innocent and just occasionally uses the house where my kidnapper took me? Maybe someone figured out that she doesn't go there that often and used it for their own devices?"

"Natalie, don't be crazy. Everything links back to her and there's got to be a reason why. It's proper to think everyone innocent until proven otherwise, but what does your gut tell you?"

"You're right, Amanda. I just...we've lived so close to each other and she's been so nice to me that I can't figure her for a criminal."

Detective Brock spoke next, "You of all people should know that criminals don't ever look like the boogeyman. Give me a moment, I'm going to send Officer Nickles out to question Ms. Stork." He left Amanda and me in the small lab while I thought about what I would do if it were Ms. Stork who was after me. And what I would do if she weren't the culprit.

"Let's go home, Natalie. We really shouldn't be here when she's brought in. They'll call us when they find out something more."

"You're right I just...OK, let's go."

We spoke with Detective Brock on the way out and he promised to call as soon as he knew anything more. We hadn't been at Amanda's for long before he called. "Ms. Stork's gone. Everything is gone from her apartment, but Officer Nickles is on his way out to the house in the industrial park. Do you know of any of her relatives we can get in touch with if she's not there?"

"I have no idea. Everything's gone? How can that be? Amanda was just there a few hours ago. Amanda, did they have anything packed? Any boxes that you saw?"

"Nothing at all. Ms. Stork and Jeffrey seemed quite out of breath though, and there was another man there looking at all of their things. Maybe...oh no, maybe he was organizing their things to ship them somewhere. This is crazy! Do you still think she's innocent now?"

"She must have recognized Amanda and known we were on to her. Maybe you can match her DNA to someone else in the system?"

"Sure, but analyzing DNA can take days or weeks. I'll let you go and will keep you posted as soon as I hear anything else. Maybe she's hiding out at her other place. Who knows? She may not be as bright as we think she is."

Nothing Amanda suggested could settle my mind or my stomach. I clutched my hot double chocolate with marshmallows and Bailey's but I had left it untouched for too long and it was too cold now to drink. Sudoku and word search books lay on the couch beside me, a pencil in my other hand, but I was lost in thought and left them closed. A movie was playing, one of my favorites, and yet I looked only at the melted marshmallows in my mug. I wanted to voice an apology, realized I was being rude, but I knew Amanda understood what I couldn't say.

Gary came out to talk to us; I remained mute while Amanda explained why. The phone rang and I reached for it quickly but Amanda was faster and answered it, telling Detective Brock that I was too shaken to speak. He hesitated to tell her, but finally admitted they couldn't find Ms. Stork or this Jeffery fellow we had told him about. They'd continue the search, a BOLO — be on the lookout — was announced, and tomorrow they'd have more results from the DNA with which to work. He recommended that Amanda give me a sleeping pill and get me to bed; she followed his advice.

Chapter 41

In the morning, Professor Matthews called to tell me the unfortunate news that he had found nothing more to investigate. I cut the call short, telling him that the police had a lead but that I wasn't able to say what it was. Amanda was finally able to convince me to eat by making me French toast and bacon, while Gary ran to the store to get orange juice.

I ate without tasting the food and had to run to the bathroom to deposit it into the toilet. I couldn't believe I was taking this situation so badly but knew my reaction was only natural. I had thought I was trained for letting evidence lead me to seemingly innocent people and their arrest. I just couldn't believe that Ms. Stork had literally been under my nose the whole time and I had thought she was great. We easily connected, but now I wondered how real the connection was.

I heard the phone ring but didn't make any effort to stand up to get it. I knew Amanda would report all there was to know, if anything. She knocked on the bathroom door soon after I got sick to offer me orange juice and an update. I told her I'd be right out and apologized for not being able to stomach her breakfast or the desire for orange juice at the moment.

Anxious to hear what she had to say, I barely bothered to brush my teeth and almost forgot to flush the toilet before I met Gary and Amanda in the living room. I sank onto the couch and asked what was new.

"Well, Detective Brock thinks we need to move you. If Ms. Stork knows I'm your best friend, she may come looking for you here. The police still haven't found her and we need to keep you out of harm's way."

"But she doesn't seem to want to hurt me?"

"I know that's what it seems like..."

"But she also seemed innocent of any wrongdoing. I get it. I'll move out. I'll go —"

"Don't tell us. Call Detective Brock back and have him pick you up. He'll take you wherever he feels is best. Pick up a prepaid cell phone on the way and call us, but don't give us your number. That way if Ms. Stork does call or show up we really have nothing to give her. Don't worry, we'll be fine. Gary is staying home with me and we have Detective Brock's direct number."

I called Charlie to tell him that I was ready to be picked up. My tears were falling so slowly I barely noticed them, and Amanda walked over to wipe them off my cheek. When I hung up, she hugged me and attempted to reassure me that everything would be sorted out very soon. Wanting very much to believe her, I just nodded ever so slightly.

Packing my belongings in silence, I completely broke down and began blubbering an apology to Amanda. "I didn't want you to get mixed up in this and I blamed Gary in the very beginning. I'm not being a good friend and you're being the best friend anyone could have. I feel terrible. I hope Ms. Stork leaves you alone. You need to be safe too. I'll wait outside, I —"

"Oh no you won't, not alone anyway. Don't worry about Gary and me right now. Your safety is the concern. I don't know how many times you have to be told that before you stop apologizing. If you want to wait outside, Gary and I are coming with you."

Instead of answering I grabbed my packed bag, put on my shoes, and went out to the front step. Gary and Amanda followed me closely and sat on the railing, their backs to the street while I stood. My gasp put the two on alert and they asked what was wrong.

"Ms. Stork just drove by, maybe. I dunno, maybe it was my imagination. I'm certainly not myself lately."

"You don't need to be. What's happening to you would cause anyone to be fearful." Gary was right. I just didn't want to fully comprehend the situation I was in, even though its harshness was crashing down hard. Detective Brock pulled up and I said my brief goodbyes.

"Not goodbye, Natalie. See you later," Amanda said back.

Unable to voice a response, I got into the car and waved from the window. "Where are you taking me?"

"I talked to Professor Matthews and he offered to let you stay in his spare room."

"But his family..."

"All agreed and I think that's the safest place for you, especially over the weekend. Ms. Stork probably won't ever think you would stay there, and Brian promises to stay home with you in case she does figure it out. I'd offer my place but there's not a whole lot of room."

"I'd never ask you to do that..."

"That's why it would be an offer." In minutes we pulled into the driveway of Professor Matthews' house, one I'd been in a few times for study sessions with other classmates. "I picked up a prepaid phone for you and I'll only call you on that. Use it when you call any of your friends so that whoever is after you can't trace you."

Brian was out on his step and began walking to the car. No one was allowing me much time alone, but for once, I was thankful. Detective Brock drove away after ensuring he'd call as soon as he found Ms. Stork and brought her in.

Chapter 42

It took days, but the police finally found Ms. Stork at her stepsister's place two towns away. Detective Brock was in the process of questioning her as Professor Matthews drove me to the station. His family had been so kind to me but I had other things on my mind and didn't think to thank him. There would be time for that after this was all figured out.

I got to the police fifteen minutes after finding out Ms. Stork had been brought in and only forty-five minutes behind her arrival. I was refused access to observe the interview so I waited in the lobby through the entire two-hour session, unfortunately without updates. Professor Matthews had to go, so I called Amanda and asked her to wait with me. She arrived with Gary and schoolbooks, promising to stay for as long as she could, admitting that she was well behind in her schoolwork and desperately needed to catch up. Professor Matthews promised Gary he could stay with me and that he wouldn't be penalized for his absence in class. When Detective Brock finally made his appearance, Gary and I were waiting, as Amanda had returned to school.

"Natalie, you need to hear what I have to say alone, but I think you'll need Gary to drive you home."

"What? Did she confess? What's going on?"

"Please come to my office. Susan, can you get Gary a coffee and maybe a book from our forensics lab for him to read?"

"Sure thing."

I didn't even bother to look back at Gary as I made my way to Detective Brock's office. Nothing could have prepared me for what was to come.

Taking a seat, I struggled to stay silent until Detective Brock began to explain. Instead of giving me answers, he began with more questions. "Natalie, do you remember your parents ever discussing why you were an only child?"

"What are you talking about? I want answers, not an interrogation. I thought you had to tell me something?"

"I do, Natalie, I'm sorry. I am trying to make this as easy for you as possible. Before we found Ms. Stork, more test results came in that we wanted to reconfirm before sharing with you. It seems you're related to Ms. Stork."

"Test the DNA again, something's wrong. I never met Ms. Stork before moving into her apartment building. There's some mistake." My memory drifted back in time, trying to remember why my parents told me I would never have a brother or sister. All I remembered was them considering adopting another child but deciding against it. And then suddenly I remembered something that had seemed insignificant at the time…

…My mother was embracing me, hugging me tighter than ever before, when my dad came in the room. I was about five years old and had just come home from school. It seemed like an ordinary day but a special moment between my parents and me. "What did I do, mommy?"

"Oh, sweetie. It's just…I just…we love you so much."

"You're our miracle baby, Natalie. We want you to always remember that and know that we love you very much."

"I know. I love you both, too. Always 'member that please." They had chuckled, but I recalled seeing sadness in their eyes, though I wasn't able to recognize the emotion at such a young age. I couldn't make sense of it then, or now, but thought maybe I would soon by the way Charlie was leading the conversation.

"Natalie, I don't know how to tell you this."

"Just tell me. I've been through enough, don't you think? Is Ms. Stork my stalker or what?" His phone rang at that moment and he excused himself, answering it.

"Uh huh, oh, thank God. Send her in please." Disconnecting the line, he told me there was someone here to see me just as there was a soft knock on the door. What startled me was seeing the woman who opened it. I would never forget her kind eyes and soft face.

"Officer Fraser! What are you doing here?" I wanted to get out of the chair, to hug her and tell her my new horror, but my legs felt squishy and I suddenly realized she knew why I was there.

"Detective Thompson now. It's been a long time. I wish we were meeting again under very different circumstances."

"You're telling me," I tried to say lightly but the words came out like lead. "What brings you here?"

"Detective Brock was hoping that what he needed to tell you would come out better from someone you knew. Someone who dealt with your parents' case."

"Has it been solved?"

She took the seat next to me while thanking Charlie for giving her this opportunity. She sat so she could look me straight in the eye and laid her hand on mine. "It has, but we never could have done it without you. I just wish it hadn't been solved this way."

"What way?"

"With you being stalked, with you discovering so much."

"I haven't discovered anything. What's going on here? Why isn't anyone just telling me the truth?" I looked from Detective Brock to Detective Thompson and back. Then Detective Thompson spoke.

"The tests aren't wrong — you are related to Ms. Stork. She's your birth mother."

Bursting into tears, I began screaming that they were lying. I couldn't fathom anyone being my mother except the woman I'd always known as my mother: the woman who hugged me when I was five and said I was her miracle child, who made me cookies, and who met me at the door every day after school. The woman I grew to be seven years old with and the woman I found on the kitchen floor bleeding and dead less than an hour after her murder. "No. No, it can't be. That's impossible. I know my mother. She was murdered. Tell me who murdered her."

Chapter 43

"I know this has to be hard on you."

"You do? No, you have no idea. It's *not* hard, because I know it's not true. Maybe she's an aunt who I never met, a distant cousin — if she's related at all. Ms. Stork is not my mother!"

"DNA has confirmed it, Natalie," Detective Brock said so softly I barely heard. "Ms. Stork admitted to everything."

"She murdered my parents?"

"It was an accident. She was furious with them, wanted to have you back, but they refused. They knew what was best for you and stood up for you plenty of times. That day, the day of their deaths, was a day they underestimated a mother's conviction." I was still shaking my head; none of this was making any sense, but I saw no doubt in Detective Thompson's eyes.

"Your parents got a restraining order against her. They wanted nothing to do with Ms. Stork and certainly didn't want you finding out."

"Finding out what? Would someone just tell me what's going on?" Detective Brock told me they had said enough and that I would have to wait until morning to hear any more. "You've got to be kidding me! I'm the victim here and you're treating me like a criminal. Why won't you tell me what's going on?"

"We think it's best for you to speak directly with Ms. Stork, Natalie. Detective Brock has set up a meeting between the two of you for tomorrow. Her lawyer won't allow it to happen any sooner. I'm going to drive you home and we'll discuss ideas for questions, as I think it's best you be prepared — and, Natalie, be prepared for the worst."

"I need proof..."

"You'll get more answers tomorrow. We're investigating further, but at this point we don't believe Ms. Stork has reason to lie."

"Bullshit she doesn't. She's trying to get sympathy, but she's looking to the wrong person." I stared at Detective Thompson and then Detective Brock, and realized I wouldn't get anywhere by arguing so I stood up and said, "Fine. I'll have Gary take me home, though. I'll be back tomorrow at eight in the morning. Make sure everything is set up." I wanted to slam the door on my way out but refrained. My frustration and confusion could not be dulled with the slam of a door.

Gary stood up quickly and rushed to me, I pushed him away, and then apologized for doing so. He stretched his arms, indicating he wanted to hug me and I pushed him away harder, not apologizing that time. I wasn't myself; he knew that and forgave me without even knowing why I was so upset. I needed to be alone, to think about what I had been told. "Drop me off at the cemetery, please."

"Natalie, it's late, why don't you just come home. Amanda is waiting to hear the news."

"Cemetery. I need to talk to my parents." I had to be rude, I couldn't think about being anything but direct.

"Fine, but I'm not just leaving you there. I'm going with you. I'll be close by you the whole time." I had to agree; otherwise I knew he wouldn't take me to my parents. When we arrived at the cemetery I made sure Gary was out of earshot before I broke down.

Kneeling between my parents' headstones, I cried while reflecting on my childhood with them. In hindsight everything became clearer, but at the same time became murkier than I had ever remembered. Of course, I was seven when my parents were murdered, still innocent and trusting of everyone, especially the people I had thought were my parents. Now, with everything that was happening, I couldn't believe just how stupid I had been as a kid. Maybe I had Ms. Stork to blame for that, if she really was my birth mother.

I didn't realize how late it was or how long I had been at the cemetery until my ringing phone startled me. The clock on my phone read 1:00 a.m., while the phone number indicated that Professor Matthews was calling. I hesitated to answer, but concluded it was something important because he was calling so late. "Natalie, are you all right? I just spoke with my wife and she said you never made it home."

"Excuse me, I never even thought to call. I'm with Gary at the cemetery. He'll take me back to Amanda's so I don't wake your family. Why are you up so late?"

"I'm still at the school. I just found something that might be important. I know I should bring it in to Detective Brock, but I thought I'd let you see it first. Amongst the dirt and rubble from the Arm Farm there was a tiny locket with a picture of a baby in it alongside a young woman. Do you know anything about it?"

"Nothing at all. Just take it to Detective Brock. I don't have the stamina to continue wracking my brain with these things. Good night, Brian, thanks for calling." I was so overwhelmed that I didn't even remember hanging up, walking to the car, or arriving at Amanda and Gary's. At 5:00 a.m., however, I was wide-awake and anxious to get to the police station even though the interview wasn't until 8:00 a.m. I thought of taking Amanda's car while she slept but knew the decent thing to do was to wait until she woke up, and that's what I managed to do.

Thank goodness she was up at 6:00 a.m., having decided it may take some time to wake me and get me ready. She found me staring out her living room window while leaning with my belly on the back of her sofa. "Are you sick?"

"Yeah, but nothing you'll need to clean up. What is going on, Amanda?"

"I have no idea. Do you want to tell me what you found out last night?"

"Oh God, yes. I can't believe I didn't explain anything to you yet. I just..."

"You certainly don't need to justify your actions. It must have been horrible, must *be* horrible going through all of this."

"You don't know a quarter of it..." I explained everything that had been uncovered. "Crazy thing is that I've finally convinced myself that Ms. Stork is telling the truth. She is my mother."

"No, Natalie. You spent seven great years with your mother and unfortunately she died way too early. No one will ever take her place."

"But Ms. Stork gave birth to me. Why didn't my parents ever tell me they weren't my birth parents?"

"At seven years old? How could they explain that to you so that you would understand, but not be mad?"

"I could never be mad at them."

"You are now, aren't you? Just a little bit...I think they did the right thing. They couldn't have known how dangerous Ms. Stork would become. Don't let this bother you. You're a great person no matter who birthed you."

"That's easy for you to say. You know who your parents are and they are still alive." I may have sounded jealous and bitter, but that was not my intention.

"Don't blame me because my parents are still alive, Natalie. I know you're going through so much right now so I've forgiven you for your actions lately. I'm through being blamed for you turning out so wonderfully despite the fact that you have a bad history."

"I know. I'm not thinking. I'm just continually apologizing for my actions instead of thinking them through.

Please erase all of my actions from your memories and still be my friend when this is all over, no matter what I do."

"Deal. Go get in the shower and then I'll drive you to the station. Did you want breakfast? You really should eat something."

"I can't — eat, I mean. I'll go shower but if you let me borrow your car I can drive myself to the station."

"Absolutely not, I'm driving and I'll be there when you're done."

Amanda was still waiting when I was finished meeting with Ms. Stork, which meant she sat in the police station lobby for just over four hours. Nothing said 'true friend' more than her patience, with me and otherwise. I had spent three-quarters of the past few hours speaking with Ms. Stork, and took the rest of the time to recover from all the information I had been given.

"She's my mother."

Amanda stood and gave me the tightest hug I'd had in a very long time, which made my tears fall once again. She didn't say anything; there really wasn't anything for her to say, and I decided to stay silent as well. We went out to her car where Amanda waited fifteen minutes before speaking, having difficulty composing herself over my news.

"Do you want to tell me what happened?"

"The locket that Professor Matthews found was hers. She gave it to me." I held it up, barely holding on to the chain while dangling the open locket for Amanda to see. "That's me."

Amanda briefly looked at it, telling me it was OK to cry it out and asking me where I wanted to go. "I don't care right now."

"Natalie...."

"No, really. I...I need to absorb all this. Just take me back to my apartment, I'll be safe now."

"Should you be alone?"

"Yes, I need to be."

Dropping me off, she told me to call as soon as I felt up to talking. She said she'd plug her cell phone in, turn the ringer up high, and wait by it until I called. When I arrived at my bedroom, I collapsed into bed, too confused to realize how relieved I was to be safe at home in my own bed, the meeting with my birth mother replaying itself on my ceiling.

Chapter 44

"Natalie, thank you for coming." She had begun so
politely, like what she was about to tell me was nothing more than
a story she had read. I was thankful to see Krista and Stephen
sitting on my side of the table, with Ms. Stork in handcuffs beside
her lawyer on the other side. As I couldn't take my eyes off the
woman, I was relieved to sense Detective Brock and Detective
Thompson take seats on the other side of me.

I just sat there, looking at Ms. Stork's hands chained to
the table, too afraid to look in her eyes for fear of deep
recognition, but her hands also told the story. They were so much
like my own, much more than my mother's or father's — or at
least, the parents I'd known until this moment.

"I know this must be difficult. You must feel —"

"You don't know me at all, how can you know how I
feel?"

"That's where you're wrong —"

"Because you stalked me for a couple of weeks you think
you know me?" She looked surprised when I was finally able to
lift my head to meet her look.

"Did the police not tell you? I've been following you
your entire life. I couldn't just let you go as I thought I could. I
had to know who you became, had to know where you ended up
and how you got there."

"Who are you?"

"Natalie, I'm your mother."

"No, my mother died a long time ago, I..."

"She adopted you. Your parents came to me, met me through a friend, your dad pretended he was meeting me for the first time and we made arrangements for them to take care of you until I could get back on my feet. I was confused, young and your father...he was married and completely in love so it was impossible for us to be together.

"When we found out I was pregnant, your father was thrilled but horrified. Shortly after that he broke it off with me, told me he couldn't be with me but promised to support the child for as long as I needed.

"I didn't want his money though I needed it desperately. If he wasn't going to be with me, with his first-born, I...well...I didn't want to go through with the pregnancy."

"You bitch!"

"I know, but as I said, I was alone and confused. I didn't know how to raise a child by myself and really didn't care to. We did take all the proper precautions but it turned out we were that "point oh-one percent" exception to birth control studies.

"I loved your father, deeply and completely, so I couldn't bear to be with anyone else."

"What's his name? Where is he now?" I didn't realize I believed the story until I asked the question. I was furious that she ignored my questions and continued at her own pace.

"I finally decided to have you. I couldn't actually see myself killing an innocent child before he or she saw light. I knew I'd have to put you up for adoption, and hated having to do that too. Who knew what type of people would finally adopt you —"

"Good people, the best parents I could ever ask for."

"But I didn't know that when I was just six months pregnant. When I met your father's wife, I was seven months along, as big as a watermelon and still suffering with morning sickness and sinus congestion. Through a stuffy nose and watery eyes, I was still able to see the love the couple shared, the mother she would become, and understood it was for the best.

"Your father and his wife were at the hospital when you were born. I called them when I knew my contractions were the real thing and they were waiting for me when I arrived. They came into the delivery room and helped me through the process. Both of them were terrific, from what I can remember. Your father's wife kept bringing me water while your father held my hand.

"I didn't know how much your father's wife knew. I couldn't bring myself to ask, even when she left the room. It was your father's decision to tell her or not. I wouldn't ruin that."

"What are you talking about? Knew about what? Ruin what?"

"They didn't want me to meet you. They were afraid, understandably so, that I would change my mind. I thought about it more than a thousand times but knew, in my heart, that they were the best parents for you. They could offer you so much more than I could — just look at where you ended up, what a great person you turned out to be — and they only had you for seven years."

"I went out to the Arm Farm because I knew your mother's body, or at least parts of it, were there. I needed to thank her for the values she taught you. I wanted to shake her hand when she was alive but couldn't bring myself to do it with her sinewy dead hand. Then I figured you might notice the dirt around her having been freshly stepped on and had to try to hide it."

It was so much information to take in. She kept dodging my questions, avoiding eye contact when I asked them. She gave me so much information while leaving so many important aspects out. My hand was sore from banging the table in complete frustration. Krista suggested several times that we take a break, but I couldn't. Ms. Stork's lawyer advised her against speaking so freely, but she went against him and continued.

"Your name — they named you after me. Not your first name, of course, but your middle. Olivia. Mine is Olive. Did you know that? I wasn't sure if I ever gave you my first name, as I tried to be careful not to. I didn't want you to know all of this, even after your parents passed away —"

"Passed away? You murdered them, Ms. Stork! There's nothing peaceful about that; they didn't "pass," they were catapulted. Get to your point."

"I wanted to take your picture even though they had insisted I have nothing to do with you at all. When you were seven, you were so sweet and I needed another picture. Just your school picture was all I wanted. I called, but your parents wouldn't speak to me and didn't return any of my messages. I pleaded, I begged, I went to a lawyer to discuss my rights. Your parents were threatened, of course, when I told them I was talking to a lawyer. They thought I was seeking custody, nothing as simple but as precious as a picture.

"It was all I really wanted. I didn't want you in my custody. I still wasn't in a stable relationship and my life really had no room for me to be a full-time mom. That's why I stayed away when they died. I could have easily come in and taken you away from your friends and adoptive family, but I couldn't take that risk.

"When I showed up at your house, only your mother was home. I caught her in the middle of making cookies and cutting up carrots at the same time. She was a multi-tasker through and through. I guess you have to be in order to be a great mother. It's too bad she wasn't able to have her own children. She so badly wanted more and had wanted a child for many years before finally adopting you.

"So I knocked on the door and she answered, but immediately slammed it shut when she saw that it was me. I was too quick. She didn't have time to lock the door, so I forced it open. I told her I didn't mean any harm. I didn't, really. I just thought she would finally see how important it was for me to have a recent picture of you.

"She told me you'd be home soon and that I had to go. She wouldn't let me talk, wouldn't give me time to explain. I tried shouting and because of our volume, I didn't hear your dad come home. He told me to go to the living room and that he'd meet me there.

"I complied, figuring I could level with him more effectively. I didn't realize your mother was in the doorway when we were talking. I didn't see the knife still in her hand when she ran towards me. At the last minute I got out of the way..."

"What are you saying?" I was terrified of what she was going to say next and equally as terrified that it would be more lies. I still couldn't completely believe everything Ms. Stork was revealing.

Chapter 45

"The knife hit your father instead. She didn't do it on purpose. I don't think she even intended to hurt me with it, but when I moved out of the way he tried to catch her. When he reached for her, she collapsed into him and the knife, with carrot slices and all, buried in his chest. She took it out, not thinking, but instinctively believing removing the knife would help. It only made the situation worse.

"She began weeping and then ran to the kitchen to call 911. She left him to die in the living room. I guess they found his body collapsed over the coffee table and he just lost too much blood. My only thoughts were of you. I wasn't thinking straight. I picked up the knife she dropped by your father's side and went after her. I didn't even think about his safety. I only wanted to talk, to explain that he loved you and that was why he left me."

"You're trying to have me believe my father had an affair with you and is my biological father? I can't, I won't. He loved my mother so much he..."

"Natalie, he cheated on her. We were both away on business. He was so distraught over the fact that she couldn't bear his child. We met at a bar and hadn't seen each other since college even though we both lived in Boston, so we caught up. I consoled him and the rest is history. I guess he didn't tell your mother. It was our little secret.

"We struggled then. She was furious with your father. I couldn't let her call 911 because she'd blame his murder on me. I was holding the knife — my fingerprints were all over it."

"You killed both of them. Don't blame anyone else for your stupidity."

"Natalie, I have no reason to lie to you anymore. I'm going to jail. I'll serve my time. I just wanted to clear the air between us so you can begin to forgive me."

"Never." I got up to leave. I wanted to be as far away from this woman as possible, but her next words stopped me.

"I love you."

"Then why did you give me up? Don't give me this bull about knowing what was best for me. Obviously you didn't believe it yourself because you felt the need to follow me and torture me from behind closed doors."

"I truly believe I wasn't the best mother for you, but I needed to be as close to you as your parents would allow."

I left then. Without another word I walked to Detective Brock's office, sat down, and wept. I wept for my parents, the two people I loved most in this world. For my mother, who never knew my dad had cheated on her but would have forgiven him for doing so. For myself, for finally being free of Ms. Stork.

I cried now, in my bed, for all of the same things and more. Freedom came at a price: a high price, but one that I had to pay. Detective Brock explained that Jeffery had only done what his girlfriend asked him to do. When he rented the car and handed her the keys, he'd had no idea what she was going to do. He, too, would have his day in court but for some strange reason I believed he acted without provocation, without knowing what he was actually doing and why. Ms. Stork could be very convincing and conveniently left out a lot of important pieces when she saw fit.

Arm Farm

I cried all the way to my car, while driving to the Arm Farm, and during the time it took me to return to the place where we had found my mother's arm. As I stood looking at the ground, I felt something drop from my numb hand. Looking down to see the open locket, I knew what I had to do.

And as I walked back through the valley of the shadow of arms, I quickened my pace, dried my tears and prayed quietly. "…Stay inside me as I dare to tread, be beside me in case I stumble. Dear God, guide me through this…"

Sarah Butland is the author of two other books. Her first book was a children's book titled Sending You Sammy and was written when she realized how easy it was to do her part for helping children be and stay healthy.

Brain Tales – Volume One is a collection of short stories for teenage and young adult readers.

She currently resides in Moncton, New Brunswick, Canada with her husband, son, a cat named Russ and a dog named Corona. She hopes this is only the beginning of a long writing career.